THE
ROOKIE
ARRIVES

THE ROOKIE ARRIVES

THOMAS J. DYGARD

MORROW JUNIOR BOOKS / NEW YORK

Author's Note

The Kansas City Royals are a real baseball team. So are the Detroit Tigers, the New York Yankees, and all the other teams mentioned in this book. But the characters and happenings are entirely fictional, not based in any way on real people or real events.

Copyright © 1988 by Thomas J. Dygard
All rights reserved.
No part of this book may be reproduced
or utilized in any form or by any means, electronic
or mechanical, including photocopying, recording or by any
information storage and retrieval system, without
permission in writing from the Publisher.
Inquiries should be addressed to
William Morrow and Company, Inc.
105 Madison Avenue
New York, NY 10016.
Printed in the United States of America.
1 2 3 4 5 6 7 8 9 10
Library of Congress Cataloging-in-Publication Data
Dygard, Thomas J.
The rookie arrives / Thomas J. Dygard.
p.   cm.
Summary: Cocky Ted Bell moves from being star of his high school
baseball team directly into playing in the major leagues and finds
that he has a lot to learn before becoming the world's greatest
third baseman.
ISBN 0-688-07598-3 (lib. bdg.)
[1. Baseball—Fiction.]   I. Title.
PZ7.D9893Ro 1988
[Fic]—dc19
87-26238
CIP

for Joel Adam Dygard

THE
ROOKIE
ARRIVES

CHAPTER

1

By the time Ted Bell stepped off the airplane in Chicago to join the Kansas City Royals in the middle of their series with the White Sox, everyone in the world knew they were about to witness the emergence of the greatest third baseman in the history of baseball.

Well, at least everyone in Ted Bell's world—his teammates and friends back at Genoa High School in Oklahoma; most of the townspeople; the major league scouts who were always dropping in to watch him play; the metals engineer who sat next to him on the plane; and now the flight attendant, who was smiling her farewells to the departing passengers at Chicago's O'Hare Airport.

Carrying a green canvas duffel bag stuffed with underwear, socks, a couple of sport shirts, an extra pair of slacks, and his glove, with his favorite bat strapped to the outside, Ted shuffled along in the line toward the exit of the airplane.

He was traveling light—just enough clothes from the recently ended Genoa High days to last until he learned the proper attire of a major league baseball player. Then he would buy his wardrobe. That was what part of the bonus money was for.

"Good luck," the flight attendant said with a smile when he reached her at the door.

Ted grinned at her. "Luck? I don't need luck."

She nodded absently and turned her smile to the next passenger coming along behind Ted.

Ted stepped through the door of the airplane onto the exit ramp and began striding toward the waiting area.

Everyone had been wishing him luck the last couple of days—his teammates and friends at Genoa High; Coach Greene; Doc Gaylord at the drugstore; even his father, who disapproved of Ted's decision to forgo college for a Kansas City Royals contract.

But Ted knew that luck had nothing—nothing at all—to do with the way he played baseball.

It wasn't luck that placed his batting average at .680 in his just-finished senior year at Genoa High. It was a remarkable pair of eyes—he could see the stitches clearly on a fast ball coming at him—and strong hands and wrists and shoulders, and the smooth coordination of every muscle in his body when he swung a bat. Ted knew the ingredients of a .680 batting average. And luck was not one of them.

There was no luck involved in playing a flawless season in the field—not one error in the twenty-one games of the Genoa High season. Bunts, line drives, pop-ups, scorching grounders—he had gobbled them all up without a single miscue in the entire season. Quick hands, quick feet, a strong arm, those were the ingredients of flawless fielding, not luck.

It wasn't luck, either, that had him landing in Chicago to put on a Royals uniform and play in the major leagues instead of riding a bus to some bush-league town to begin a year or two of "seasoning."

The major league scouts who came around to see him play all told him that he should expect it—"seasoning." They all said he needed a year, or maybe two, in the minor leagues to develop his batting eye and his fielding touch in the professional game. They pointed out that Joe DiMaggio had played minor league ball and that Mickey Mantle had spent time in the minor leagues. So had Bo Jackson. They all said that playing every day in Charleston or Louisville or Springfield—or somewhere—would be more beneficial to his career than riding a bench in the major leagues. But Ted did not want to play at Charleston or at Louisville or at Springfield. Ted wanted the major leagues. And he did not intend to ride a bench in the major leagues. He intended to play. And now, right away, not in a year or two after choking on the dust in some bush-league town.

Ted told all the visiting scouts the same thing: "I may as well go to college and play there as go somewhere in the minors. You're just wasting a draft choice if you think I'm going to the minors."

Most of the scouts listened, nodded, and walked away. And Ted knew that each time, somewhere, in a computer room far away from Genoa, an electronic signal erased his name from a list. But he didn't care. He was holding out for the major leagues now, not Charleston or Louisville or Springfield.

As the scouts departed, one by one, Coach Greene told Ted that he was making a mistake. No major league club was going to guarantee an untried rookie a spot on the roster. It was too big a gamble—a chance the clubs did not want to take, did not have to take. Ted might be good, but he was not the only good baseball player on the scouts' lists. There were others, willing to prove themselves in the minors before getting a chance in the major leagues. But Ted held his ground.

Through it all Ted's father said nothing. He had made his position clear at the outset. He urged Ted to choose college. But he said he would not dictate that Ted must turn his back on a baseball contract and attend college. Mr. Bell did not need to say more. Ted knew full well where his parents stood. His father was the president of Genoa Community College, and his mother, a librarian, headed the children's division at the Genoa Public Library. Ted had grown up with the assumption that he would go to college. So his father said nothing more, but he clearly viewed the disappearance of each scout as one more encouraging sign that the immediate future held college—and not professional baseball—for his son.

But not all the scouts shrugged and walked away. Buck Sutton, balding, lanky, and stooped, always with a toothpick in his mouth, kept coming over from his home in Tulsa to watch Ted play. He kept coming, even after Ted told him that he would settle for nothing less than the guarantee of a place on a major league roster. Buck Sutton, whose playing days with the New York Yankees ended before Ted was born, always nodded noncommitally—and then returned for another look. Buck Sutton thought he saw something in the strong, quick, young third baseman who never erred, the powerful young hitter who slammed the ball all over the lot. He thought he saw greatness. And that's what he told his employers, the Kansas City Royals.

The Royals finally agreed—a trial in the major leagues through the end of the current season but no promises about what might happen after that.

The limit on the guarantee did not bother Ted. He figured that the four months remaining in the season provided ample time to lock up the third base job. No problem at all. He would simply hit and field—and win the job. No problem.

And so the Royals drafted Ted Bell, and on the afternoon of his graduation from Genoa High, his frowning father—signing for his eighteen-year-old son—put his signature on a Kansas City Royals contract. An expressionless Buck Sutton watched.

Ted was to join the Royals in Chicago three days later. And luck had nothing to do with it.

Ted stepped out of the exit ramp and stopped. A man behind him bumped into him, then moved on without speaking. Ted opened his mouth to say, "Excuse me," but he said nothing to the man's departing back. Ted stepped to the side, outside the flow of people emerging from the exit ramp. He looked around the waiting area. It was jammed with people. Some were greeting each other. Some were chattering at each other. Some were slouched in chairs, reading newspapers or just sitting and staring. Beyond the waiting area, Ted saw throngs of people moving up and down the concourse. There were so many of them that they almost seemed to be the parts of one rippling body flowing by. Back home, the Genoa airport was a single landing strip with a little corrugated metal building. The only person always there was Harry Slidell, who offered airplane rides for twelve dollars and sold gasoline to airplane owners—and he was usually alone. The Tulsa airport, where Ted had begun his flight to Chicago, had seemed a pretty big and busy place. But in this one, Ted figured, everyone in the Tulsa airport could pass by every minute.

Ted grinned at the scene before him and said aloud, "Hello, big city. I'm here."

He walked through the waiting area and into the concourse and glanced right, then left. He saw a sign with an arrow: TERMINAL. He followed the arrow.

Some of the people coming at him in the concourse eyed the baseball bat strapped to his bag. Then they stared at his face with open curiosity. They wondered if they had seen the face—strong jaw, clean-shaven, clear skin except for a few freckles under the eyes, longish hair of a reddish-brown tint—staring out at them from some sports page.

"Not yet," Ted said to himself. "But you will."

A small boy with a woman said, "Look, Mommy, a baseball player!"

Ted grinned and winked at the boy.

He came out of the concourse and into the main terminal on the second level. Through the glass walls he saw a tangle of cars in the driveway outside. They were double-parked, even triple-parked. Marge Einstadt, who patrolled the main street of Genoa checking the time left on parking meters, would have ticketed them all. But a policeman in the center of the driveway was paying no attention. He was waving the moving cars through. Most of the parked cars were standing with the trunk lid up.

People around them were shaking hands and kissing. In the crowd of cars Ted saw no taxis.

He walked to a down escalator and rode it to the ground level. Crowds of people were swarming around a moving ramp loaded with luggage of all descriptions. No two bags were alike. The row of luggage snaked its way through the crowd, with a piece occasionally being lifted off and carried away. A tiny woman, about the age of Ted's mother, was trying to wrestle a large bag off the moving ramp. Ted walked over and lifted the bag to the floor for her. She looked at him in surprise, said nothing, and shoved the bag away on its little wheels. Ted shrugged and walked to the glass doors and saw a row of taxis parked outside.

He stepped through the doors and walked across the sidewalk. The air outside was hot and muggy, like an oven after the walk through the air-conditioned terminal. The late-afternoon sun put a bright glare on everything. Ted blinked in the sunlight and walked toward a cabbie leaning on the front fender of his cab.

"Comiskey Park?" he asked.

"Yes, sir." The cabbie came off the fender, walked around the front of the cab, and got in behind the wheel.

Ted opened the back door and tossed his canvas bag, with the bat attached, into the backseat and climbed in behind it.

"You a ball player?" the driver asked as he wheeled

the taxi past the rows of terminals and around the O'Hare Hilton Hotel and the huge parking deck, heading for the Kennedy Expressway into the city.

"Yep."

"White Sox?"

"Nope. I'm the new third baseman for the Royals," Ted said. Then he added, "The Kansas City Royals."

"New third baseman, huh? What's your name?"

"Ted Bell."

"Ted Bell," the driver repeated. He leaned forward and to his right, glancing at Ted in his rearview mirror. "What's happening to Lou Mills?"

Ted had heard the question before. His friends in Genoa—and even Doc Gaylord—had asked the question. As a matter of fact, the question always was asked whenever Ted announced he was going to play third base for the Royals. What's happening to Lou Mills?

Lou Mills, a fifteen-year veteran at third base for the Royals, was a legendary name in baseball. People compared him to George Kell and Brooks Robinson when they talked about great third basemen. Lou Mills had won three batting championships. Twice he had been named the American League's most valuable player. He was a fixture on All-Star teams.

But he was thirty-five or thirty-six years old now, maybe older. He was nearing the end of the road as an active player. There was no denying it.

Ted himself had asked the question once: What's happening to Lou Mills? Buck Sutton had not answered. The elderly scout had responded with only a shake of his head. Ted did not know whether Buck Sutton was indicating he didn't know the answer or was refusing to answer. Maybe he was telling Ted not to ask. Ted did not press for an answer. It didn't matter. The important point was that Ted Bell was going to be the new third baseman for the Kansas City Royals.

"I don't know what's happening to Lou Mills," Ted said.

"They trading him? I wish the Sox could get him."

"I don't know if they're trading him or what."

"He's not old enough to retire. He's got some years left."

"I guess so."

"What did you say your name was again?"

"Ted Bell."

"Umm," the driver said and, without further conversation, turned onto the Kennedy Expressway and picked up speed.

Ted settled back and watched the racing cars weave from lane to lane, and ahead he saw the outline of the city. The traffic going the other way, away from the city, was heavier and moving slowly. He figured the heavy outgoing traffic was carrying people home to the suburbs at the end of their working day in the city. He looked at his wristwatch: four forty-five. More than two hours to game time. He had plenty of time.

Ted leaned forward to ask the driver how much farther they had to go, and suddenly he saw the large sign: WHITE SOX.

"There she is," the driver said. "Home of the South Siders."

"You a White Sox fan?"

"You bet."

The driver wheeled off the expressway and up the exit ramp onto city streets, approaching the venerable ball park.

Ted, looking at a major league baseball park for the first time in his life, felt a sense of—what?—well, surprise, and a tinge of disappointment. It was old and drab, not the sparkling edifice he always envisioned when he thought of a major league park. And it was smaller than he had expected.

"You want the players' entrance, I guess."

"Yeah, sure."

The driver pulled over and stopped, then slapped his flag down and turned in the seat to face Ted. "Seventeen dollars," he said.

"Seventeen dollars!"

The driver grinned. "Welcome to Chicago."

Ted pulled a shiny new leather wallet—a graduation gift from his grandmother—out of his hip pocket and extracted a twenty-dollar bill. He handed it to the driver.

When the man said, "Thank you, sir," and made no move to offer change, Ted nodded and got out of the cab.

CHAPTER

The locker room was empty except for a short, fat, bald-headed man wearing a white T-shirt and jeans, who was sorting uniforms out of a trunk. He had a friendly sort of face, one that appeared to be used to grinning and laughing. But he gave Ted a blank look. "What can I do for you?" he asked.

"I'm Ted Bell."

The man turned his face back to his work and resumed sorting uniforms. "Congratulations," he said.

"What?"

"Congratulations on being Ted Bell. Now, what can I do for you?"

"I'm the new third baseman."

"Oh—*that* Ted Bell."

"Uh-huh."

"I'm Ernie Rome, the equipment manager."

Ted nodded and waited a moment, expecting a word

of welcome. But Ernie Rome bent down into the trunk and went back to the work of sorting out uniforms. Ted shifted his weight from one foot to the other, and then said, "Well, like, where do I put my stuff . . . and get a uniform . . . and all that?"

Ernie dropped the shirt in his hand. He stared at Ted with an expression that seemed to say the interruption was an irritation. Then he walked across the locker room. He spoke as he walked. "Over here. You're number five." He gestured at a wide stall with a director's chair in front of it, and uniforms on a hanger. "The key's in the valuables box."

"Valuables box?"

"For your wallet, wristwatch, you know."

"Oh, sure."

Ernie turned to walk back to the trunk of uniforms.

"Five," Ted said. "But—"

Ernie stopped. "But what?"

"I've always worn number eleven, and I was sort of hoping . . ."

Ernie's round face took on a pained expression, as if he were recounting all the rookies of the past who had arrived wanting to name their own number.

"On this ball club, number eleven belongs to Freddie Hanover. Number five belongs to you." He paused and then added, "As long as you're around."

Ted gave the equipment manager a sharp look and

started to speak. Then he thought better of it. What did the equipment manager matter? Ernie Rome would learn soon enough who Ted Bell was, and how long Ted Bell was going to be around.

Besides, Ted was facing Ernie's departing back.

Ted placed his canvas bag on the floor inside the stall and straightened back up. He glanced across at Ernie. Maybe being the equipment manager and spending a lifetime sorting uniforms while the stars wearing the uniforms got all the headlines left a person bitter. Ted had run into his share of envy back at Genoa High—those classmates who played no sport and liked to refer to athletes derisively as "jocks," and even some of his own teammates, who seemed almost to enjoy his rare strikeouts. No, Ted had seen the Ernie Rome types before. He always shrugged them off. So he shrugged off Ernie Rome and looked around the locker room.

There wasn't much about it that looked really major league. The place could have used a coat of paint. There were a couple of clean white training tables. There were doors leading out of the locker room, probably to an office for the manager, a whirlpool room, other stuff. He saw a television set and an easy chair through one of the doors. It was a sort of lounge. Now that was something Genoa High didn't have.

On a table against the wall a cardboard box held a couple of dozen baseballs. Ted walked over and looked at the balls. They were autographed. He looked at the names—Lou Mills, Eddie Patterson, Brian Stevens, Jim Graham, Bomba Wright—names that Ted knew from the sports pages.

"Am I supposed to sign these?" Ted asked.

Ernie rolled his eyes to the ceiling. "You just got here," he said. "Don't worry about it."

Ted dropped the ball back in the box.

The door opened, and a young man, looking barely older than Ted, walked in. He was slender, small-boned, and shorter than Ted's six-foot height by several inches. He was maybe five feet eight or nine. He had a slender beak of a nose and an expression that seemed to be asking a question. His hair was blond and long—not too long—and styled to perfection, like some of the actors on television. Ted did not recognize the face. But the young man surely was a player. He walked with the fluid smoothness of an athlete. He was wearing a maroon blazer, gray slacks, a light gray turtleneck shirt, and alligator loafers.

Ted was taking in the scene when the young man spoke. "You Bell?"

"Yes. Ted Bell."

The young man smiled as he approached Ted and extended a hand. "I'm Brian Stevens," he said. "Your roommate on the road trips."

Ted knew Brian Stevens by name but not by face. He

was the Royals' second baseman and leadoff hitter. He was only in his second or third year in the majors but already had established himself as a good glove man, a crafty, if not powerful, hitter, and a speedy and smart base runner.

Ted shook hands. "Oh, well, hi," he said. "I didn't know whether or not we had roommates or a private room."

"Roommates, usually," Brian said.

"Usually?"

"Yeah, to save a buck, you know, unless you can negotiate a private room into your contract." He grinned again. "I haven't been able to do it so far—and neither have you, huh?"

"I'm kind of new at all this."

"Uh-huh. Well, I guess they put us together because we're about the same age—not too far apart, anyway. Some of the older guys"—Brian winked—"well, some of the younger guys, too, like to run around a lot on road trips, you know."

Ted didn't know. But he said, "Yeah, sure."

Brian took off his blazer and hung it on a hanger in the stall next to Ted's. Then he began to peel off the turtleneck shirt.

"I think I'll go look at the field," Ted said. He wanted to check the bumps, if any, in the dirt of the infield. He wanted to get acquainted with the clumps of grass. It was a ritual with him. His play at third base depended on knowing the way the ball was going to bounce. Some of the fields back in Oklahoma were as hard as rock and full of pebbles. He was expecting better in the major leagues. "There's plenty of time, isn't there?" he asked.

Brian's head came out of the turtleneck shirt. He smiled as if reading Ted's mind. At second base Brian had to worry about the infield dirt and grass. "Plenty," he said.

Ted walked across the room and through an opening into the tunnel leading to the dugout and the playing field. He heard voices and the crack of a bat hitting a ball.

When he emerged in the dugout, he saw a hitter, a pitcher, and a catcher at work, and two other players squatting nearby watching the hitter. Ted walked up the steps of the dugout. He turned from the players and looked at the grandstands—rows and rows and rows of seats. A dozen or so people were sprinkled around the grandstands, the early birds who knew that the warm-ups were a part of baseball. Ted was looking at the inside of a major league ball park for the first time in his life. It was a lot bigger than the pair of bleachers that flanked the field at Genoa High.

He turned back to the players. The hitter was Eddie Patterson, the Royals' first baseman. One of the players squatting near the on-deck circle was Lou Mills. The other was Boyd Hatton, one of the great sluggers of all time, now a batting coach with the Royals. Ted recognized the three of them from a hundred pictures he had seen in newspapers and sports magazines since he was a small boy. He did not recognize the pitcher, an older man with a craggy face and an angular body who looked almost the age of Ted's father. He had an easy windup and delivery. The catcher's face was hidden by his mask.

Eddie Patterson, the Royals' cleanup hitter, was suffering through a slump. Ted had read about it on the plane in the Tulsa paper. Patterson had gone 0 for 4 against the White Sox the previous night and had only one hit in his last fourteen at bats.

The pitcher sent the ball to the plate, and Patterson swung and rifled a drive on a clothesline into right center field.

Patterson was a huge man, probably around six feet five, with thick legs, broad shoulders, large arms, and a bulging stomach that surprised Ted. No wonder he was in a hitting slump. He was out of shape. Coach Greene would have flattened that stomach for him in no time.

Lou Mills stood and turned, following the flight of the ball. Then he said, "Attaway. Smooth and level. That's the way."

The pitcher served up another, and Patterson fouled it off.

From behind Ted a squeaky voice said, "Bell."

Ted turned.

Hank Quincy, the Royals' manager, was standing in the dugout, in uniform. He was a small wisp of a man, narrow of shoulder, thin-armed, bandy-legged—a funny sight in a baseball uniform—with a tanned, creased face dominated by a pair of bushy eyebrows. His eyes had the squinty look and the wrinkles of a man who had spent a lot of his life watching things happen in bright sunshine. His cap, with the KC emblem on the front, seemed a couple of sizes too large and made him look like a small boy wearing a man's cap.

Hank Quincy never played in a major league baseball game in his life. In fact, as a second baseman, he never got higher than the Class-A leagues. He was a slick fielder and quick, but he never got his batting average much beyond his weight. He saw that he was going nowhere as a player, so he turned in his glove and his bat and became a coach—and then, a few years later, a manager. Eventually he worked his way into a major league manager's job. What Hank Quincy lacked in muscle he more than made up for in brain power. He was one of the best managers in the major leagues, with two World Series championships to prove it. But he was in trouble this year, with his team languishing in the lower half of the standings.

"I'm Hank Quincy," he said. His voice was high-pitched and had a bit of a crack in it, as if he had been shouting too much.

Ted stepped over the lip of the dugout, down the steps, and extended his hand.

The Kansas City manager stared at Ted's hand for a moment, seeming unsure what to do. Then he took Ted's hand. Hank Quincy had a limp handshake.

"C'mon in the office," he said, and turned into the tunnel.

Ted followed him.

When they walked through the locker room, Ted saw a couple of players changing into their uniforms. He did not recognize them. Quincy made no move to take Ted over for introductions. He led the way toward a door. Brian was nowhere to be seen. He was probably in the whirlpool room, or maybe the lounge.

In the office, a large but sparsely furnished room, Quincy walked around a desk and sat down, gesturing at the only other chair.

Ted sat down.

"I didn't ask for you," Quincy said without preamble. Then he stopped and made a funny little motion with his right hand as if to wipe out the words he had spoken. "Oh, I had no objection to drafting and signing you. You've got potential, I guess. But I didn't—and still don't— like the idea of bringing you up right at the beginning. It was a front-office decision, not mine." He paused and then said, as if putting the words in parentheses, "I had to send a catcher, a promising kid, down to Omaha to make room for you." He stopped again, watching Ted.

"Yes, sir," Ted said, then added, "I'll make you happy to have me."

Quincy nodded absently. "Maybe," he said. He got to his feet. The interview clearly was coming to an end. "Well, you watch Lou Mills out there. You might learn something."

Ted was getting to his feet. The full impact of what Quincy had said, almost as an offhand afterthought, was late in hitting him. "You mean . . . ?"

Quincy was already walking toward the door, heading out of the office, assuming that Ted was leaving, too. He stopped and turned. "What? What is it?"

Ted, still standing by the desk, said, "Do you mean that I won't be playing tonight?"

"Probably not," Quincy said, as if it didn't matter, and walked out of his office.

Ted followed him out the door and into the locker room.

CHAPTER

3

Ted sat on the bench, leaning back, legs spread out in front of him, arms folded across his chest. He stared out from under the bill of his cap at the field, bathed in light, and watched Joe Randolph, the Royals' center fielder, ground out to the second baseman. Ted turned his head and glanced at the scoreboard—one out, top of the ninth inning, the White Sox ahead, 11–0. For the Royals the game had been a disaster from the outset. The White Sox punched across three runs in the first inning, sending the starting pitcher to the showers almost before he had a chance to work up a sweat. And that was only the beginning. The White Sox then proceeded to chase two more Royals pitchers in building their eleven-run margin. Now, in the ninth inning, the lost cause was finally dragging to a close.

On the bench, virtually motionless, Ted had watched Lou Mills play third base. Mills sometimes stood with his hands on knees, alert, watching the batter. Other times he went into a catlike crouch, on his toes, hands extended, appearing ready to spring forward. He shifted position a lot between hitters—playing deep for some, moving in close for others, playing the bag sometimes, moving several steps to his left on occasion. Lou Mills, after fifteen years in the American League, knew the batters. He played where he expected them to hit the ball. Watching Mills, Ted realized he was going to need help from a teammate for a while, until he learned the hitters in the league.

If his first meeting with Lou Mills was any indication, Ted figured he could not expect much help from the veteran third baseman. It hadn't been a warm meeting. Maybe Lou Mills was bitter about seeing the end of the road as an active player with the Royals. Maybe he was determined not to like the young player who was arriving to replace him. Either way, Ted had received a cool greeting when he walked over and introduced himself in the locker room. Ted had just finished changing into his uniform. Mills, back in for a moment after trying to help Eddie Patterson find a way out of his batting slump, was looking for something in his stall. He turned at the sound of Ted's voice. He gave Ted a bland stare, a quick handshake, and the greeting of a man who doesn't care. "How are you?"

"I've always admired you," Ted said, hoping to thaw the conversation.

A short nod from Lou Mills—nothing more.

Maybe Lou Mills had seen too many rookies come and go over the years to be bothered with spending time with the latest one.

"Are you retiring, or are they going to trade you?" Ted asked.

Lou Mills blinked in surprise.

For a moment Ted regretted asking the question. It had seemed a normal enough question. But Mills looked genuinely taken aback. Was it possible the Royals had not told him about Ted Bell, the new third baseman, the booming hitter, and the miracle fielder? No, it wasn't. Surely the front office had told Lou Mills that they had signed Ted Bell and that he was joining the club in Chicago. Then why was Lou Mills acting so surprised? It was puzzling to Ted.

"I'm playing third base for the Royals," Mills said with a slight hint of a smile.

Tonight, yes, Ted thought. But there was an easy explanation, and Lou Mills should know it. Ted figured that Hank Quincy was giving him a day to settle in, get his bearings, and loosen out the kinks of the plane ride. That was all. Didn't Lou Mills know that? Or maybe Lou Mills had been told not to discuss his future. If a trade was in the works, or if he was planning to hang up his glove and retire, the Royals might have their reasons for wanting to keep pending developments quiet. But what reasons? It didn't make sense. Ted Bell was on the scene now, for all the world to see. So why the secrecy? Again Ted was puzzled.

When Lou Mills made no move to say more, Ted nodded and walked away. Mills turned back to his stall.

Now Joe Randolph, having grounded out to second base, returned to the dugout. Head down, he said nothing and seated himself. Nobody said anything to him, either.

Freddie Hanover, the Royals' shortstop, hitting eighth in the lineup, stepped into the batter's box.

Ted, shifting his eyes from Joe Randolph to Freddie Hanover, who was waggling his bat and grinding his cleats into the dirt, did not see Hank Quincy approaching. Suddenly the manager was in front of him, standing over him. "Bell, hit for Wright."

Ted straightened up on the bench. "What? Sure." He scrambled to his feet and left the dugout.

He found his bat, and another one, and stepped into the on-deck circle, swinging the two bats.

Buster Krump, pitching for the White Sox, fogged a fast ball down the middle, and Freddie, watching with his bat cocked, let it go for a called strike one.

Ted swung the bats a couple more times, cutting through the air with a ferocious chop and a full follow-through, and then knelt in the on-deck circle. He watched Buster Krump at work on the mound with an interest he had not had two minutes earlier.

Buster Krump was a veteran at his peak. He had started on the mound for the American League in the previous year's All-Star Game. Ted remembered seeing him on television. And he remembered a remark by one of the announcers: Buster Krump had been around long enough to have all the savvy a pitcher needed, but not so long as to have lost his stuff. Krump was a hard thrower, a fastballer with an exaggerated windup—a high kick and a delivery that seemed to bring the ball in from out around second base before the release. He was an intimidating figure on the mound, and he overpowered a lot of hitters.

Krump fired another fastball at the plate, and Freddie poked almost timidly at it with his bat. The ball bounded weakly toward the right side of the mound. Krump stepped over, bent, and caught the ball in his glove. He righted himself, polished the ball in the pocket of the glove for a moment, and flipped an easy throw to first base for the out.

To Ted's surprise, Freddie slowed when he saw that Krump had the ball. He was already turning for the jog back to the dugout when the ball plunked into the first baseman's mitt. Back at Genoa High, Coach Greene benched players for failing to run out an infield hit.

Ted tossed aside the extra bat and walked to the plate.

As he stepped into the batter's box he heard his name on the public-address system: "Batting for Wright—Bell!" He tapped the plate with his bat. He lifted the bat into position and fixed his eyes on Buster Krump. He shifted his feet and settled in.

"Well, well," said the White Sox catcher, squatting into position. "Fresh meat."

Ted kept his eyes on Buster Krump. He had heard catchers try to distract a hitter before and always thought the tactic was pretty amateurish, sort of kid stuff. But here it was, happening in the major leagues. He ignored the White Sox catcher, as he always had ignored all other catchers who tried to needle him. He concentrated on Buster Krump.

The pitcher was leaning forward for the signal from the catcher. Then Krump's eyes shifted to Ted, holding his bat high, unmoving. Krump seemed to study everything about Ted, from his shoes to the bill of his batting helmet. Then he looked back at the catcher, nodded slightly, and went into his windup.

First the high kick.

Then the long arm coming around, like a whip, with fingers clutching the ball.

The pitch seemed to be coming in from third base, chest-high, and headed straight for Ted's chest. Ted stood his ground, waiting. The ball curved in, still close to his chest, just below his uplifted arms, and smacked into the catcher's mitt.

Ted Bell had seen his first major league curve ball.

"Ball one!" bellowed the umpire.

Krump looked from Ted to the catcher and then back at Ted.

Ted stepped out of the box, tapped a shoe with his bat, and stepped back into the box, lifting the bat into position.

Krump was nodding at the catcher. Then he went into his windup—arms up, raring back, left foot going high, the arm coming around.

The ball came like a bullet, just above the knees and to the outside. Ted let it go by.

"*Stee-ee-rike!*" the umpire shouted.

Ted glanced back at the umpire. The pitch had looked outside to him.

The catcher flipped the ball back to Krump and said, "In this league, kid, that's what's known as nicking the corner."

Krump took his time on the mound. He played with the rosin bag. He spit a couple of times. He walked around a little bit. And when he finally leaned in for the catcher's signal, he held the pose so long that he reminded Ted of a statue.

"Watch this one," the catcher said.

Krump wound up, kicked, and brought the ball down

in a straight overhand motion—the blazing Buster Krump fastball that had made him famous, coming in high, straight down the middle.

Ted tightened his grip on the bat handle, flicked the air once with the bat, began his step forward with his left foot, and started his swing—all of it in one movement within a fraction of a second.

He felt his teeth clamp together and a little muscle in his neck jump as he brought the bat around with all the power he had. He watched the approaching ball through squinted eyes.

Bat and ball came together with a cracking sound.

Ted's swing continued until he had wrapped himself into a pretzel.

He dropped the bat, sprang back, and began the sprint toward first base, head down. Then he looked up, turned his head, and sought the ball.

He found it. The ball was a towering fly to left field.

Ted touched first base and turned.

The White Sox left fielder turned almost lazily and watched the ball leave the field of play and bounce crazily among the seats in the left field grandstand.

Ted slowed his pace and jogged to second base, then third base, and then home.

Once, between second and third, he glanced at Krump, who was turning slowly and watching Ted circle the bases.

At home plate, Ted glanced at the catcher and grinned.

"You were right," he said. "That pitch was worth watching."

In the dugout a couple of players got to their feet indifferently and touched Ted's hand as he entered and took a seat on the bench. Lou Mills was not one of them.

Hank Quincy stood at the other end of the dugout, hands on hips, watching Ted, his bushy eyebrows raised. He said nothing.

CHAPTER

4

The ringing of the telephone on the bedside table awakened Ted from a deep sleep.

He sat up with a jolt, unsure for the moment where he was. Instinctively, he reached for the telephone. Then he remembered he was in a room in the Hyatt Regency Hotel in Chicago. He glanced at the other bed—rumpled and messed up but empty. Brian Stevens, with a radio talk-show appearance on tap, had arisen, dressed, and left without waking Ted.

Ted got into a sitting position as he lifted the telephone. "Hello."

As he spoke, he slid his wristwatch around and squinted at it: eight thirty-five.

"Ted?"

"Yes."

"Did I wake you?"

"It's okay." He rubbed his eyes with his right fist, holding the telephone in his left hand. "Who is this? What is it?"

"This is Henry Jerome at the *Tulsa World*."

Ted came fully awake. "Really?" he asked. Ted had read Henry Jerome's column in the *Tulsa World* for as long as he could remember.

Jerome chuckled. "Congratulations."

"What?"

"The home run."

"Oh, yeah. Thanks."

"How does it feel—a home run in your first time at bat—and off Buster Krump?"

"Home runs always feel good."

"But this one must have been different—special."

Ted wrinkled his brow. "No, not really," he said.

"You're kidding."

"No. The pitcher throws the ball in there, and I knock it over the fence."

"The pitching is quite a bit different, though, isn't it? I mean, there's a big difference between a high school pitcher in Oklahoma and a major leaguer like Buster Krump, isn't there?"

Ted thought about the question for a moment. "Krump's curve broke sharper than anything I've ever seen."

"That's what I mean."

"But it isn't any problem." He paused. "I've only seen one pitcher's stuff. Maybe some of the others will be tougher."

"They don't come much tougher than Buster Krump."

Ted smiled at the telephone. "Well, I poled one out of the park off him, didn't I?"

"Yeah, you did," Jerome said. "You're pretty sure, then, that you're not going to have any trouble hitting major league pitching. Is that it?"

"Why should I? Same ball, same bat."

Ted heard Jerome chuckle softly, and he heard the faint sound of rustling paper as the reporter turned a page of his notebook.

"Uh, Ted . . ." Jerome said.

"Yes."

"Are you expecting to start playing third base?"

"That's what I'm here for."

"Did Quincy tell you that?"

The question put a frown on Ted's face. No, Quincy had not told him that. As a matter of fact, Quincy went out of his way to explain to Ted that he neither asked for, nor wanted, the newly signed third baseman on his roster. For the first time Ted felt a gnawing sense of doubt. What if he rode the bench, never getting his chance? No, no, surely not.

"No, Quincy didn't say that, not in so many words.

But I'm here, aren't I? I signed up to play third base for the Royals, and I'm here, so I expect to play."

"That brings up the question of Lou Mills. He's a great one. And he's a long way from finished. Where does all this leave Lou Mills?"

Ted took a deep breath. He'd been asked the question so many times. "I don't know. If he's not planning to retire, they may trade him."

"Did they tell you that—Quincy or anyone with the Royals?"

"No."

"Then what makes you think—"

"Quincy knows how long Lou Mills has been around, same as you and I do."

"Are you saying that Lou Mills is finished, over the hill?"

Ted looked at the telephone. Maybe he already had said too much. "No, I'm not saying that Lou Mills is over the hill."

"But you are saying that you expect to beat him out of the job."

"Sure, that's it."

"Uh-huh," Jerome said. "On another subject, what surprised you the most about your first major league game?"

Ted grinned into the telephone. "Well, I'll tell you— you know, that was not only the first major league game

I ever played in, it was also the first one I ever saw, except on television, and—"

"Really?"

"Yeah. And I've never seen a real major league player, and what surprised me was, well, some of these guys are fat—I mean, really fat, out of shape."

"Oh?"

"You know, beer-belly types, and that surprised me."

Jerome laughed. "Who, for instance?"

"I'd better not mention any names."

Jerome laughed again. "Okay, probably not," he agreed. There was a pause, and then he said, "Well, thanks for the conversation, Ted, and best of luck. Again, apologies for waking you up."

"No problem."

Ted replaced the receiver and sat on the side of the bed for a moment. He never had been interviewed by a newspaper reporter before. Coach Greene did not allow his players to talk to reporters, not even Buzz Kirby, sports editor of the *Genoa Mirror*.

Ted hoped he had said the right things. The reporter— Henry Jerome, of all people—certainly seemed friendly and interested. He really got a kick out of hearing about the fat players. Ted frowned briefly. Surely Henry Jerome understood that the comment was not for publication.

For a moment Ted considered giving his parents a call—to talk about the home run, to tell them about the interview, and to alert them to watch for it in the *Tulsa World*. There was just time to catch them before his father left for the day. But he decided against calling. They surely already knew about the home run from the story and the box scores in the morning paper. And they were sure to see the interview story when it appeared.

Besides, calling on the first day away from home might give the impression he was homesick.

Ted stood up and stretched his arms above his head, then walked across to the window and stared down at the city from the thirty-fourth floor. A light haze—was it smog?—hung over the city. But he could see that Chicago had a lot of very tall buildings.

He showered, shaved, and dressed quickly, and caught the elevator down to the main floor. He looked around in the huge lobby area for a familiar face—one of the Royals—and failed to find one. There must have been hundreds of faces, but all of them were strangers. With a bell captain's help he found a newsstand and bought the *Chicago Tribune* and the *Chicago Sun-Times*.

He went back to the lobby, then across it to an array of tables where people were eating breakfast. He looked around again for a familiar face and, finding none, allowed a young man in a tuxedo—a tuxedo, at nine-thirty in the morning?—to seat him at a small table against the far wall.

He scanned the menu and thought of George Pappas,

proprietor of Pappas's Cafe on Main Street back in Genoa. "If Mr. Pappas could see these prices, he'd go crazy," Ted thought.

Ted ordered breakfast and turned his attention to the newspapers.

The *Chicago Tribune* headline read, SOX HAMMER ROYALS BEHIND BUSTER'S FIVE-HITTER. The *Chicago Sun-Times* headline blared simply, SOX MAUL ROYALS. Ted looked at the pictures. One showed Buster Krump following through on a pitch. Another showed a White Sox runner in action at second base. He glanced through the stories, seeking his own name.

He found himself mentioned near the end of the *Tribune* story: "One of the five hits off Krump was a bases-empty home run by Ted Bell, a rookie making his first appearance in a pinch-hit role." The *Sun-Times* buried the mention of Ted, too: "Ted Bell, a newly arrived rookie making his first appearance, slammed a pinch-hit homer in the ninth for the Royals' only run."

Just as Ted was folding the papers to lay them aside, a voice from above said, "Reading about yourself?"

Ted looked up into the craggy face of the pitcher who had been throwing batting practice for Eddie Patterson. The craggy face wore a broad smile.

Ted started to get to his feet.

"I'm Cal Hanley. May I join you?"

"Sure." Ted sat back down.

Cal Hanley slid into a chair and took a menu from a waiter. "You've already ordered?"

"Yes."

Cal scanned the menu quickly and ordered, then turned to Ted. "That's some beginning for your major league career—a home run first time at bat, and off Buster Krump," he said with a smile. "Buster doesn't give up many of those."

Ted grinned and shrugged his shoulders. "That's what I keep hearing—that Buster Krump is pretty tough," he said. "But I poled it out of the park on him."

Cal smiled at Ted a moment without speaking. He tapped the edge of the table lightly with a forefinger. His right eyebrow went up a fraction of an inch. "You sure did," he said finally. "But, you know, you had an edge on Buster last night that you won't have next time."

Ted leaned forward. "What's that? What do you mean?"

"The White Sox didn't have a book on you."

"A book?"

"Sure, a book. Don't you know what I mean?"

Ted frowned. "No, I don't think so."

"When you walked up to the plate, you were a high school kid that nobody had ever seen before. Neither Buster Krump nor anyone else in the ball park knew how to pitch to you. High or low? Inside or outside? Curve or fastball or slider? Or what? Nobody knew. So Buster Krump did the only thing he could do with that first pitch. Do you remember it?"

"Sure. A curve."

"Right. That's the best bet against a kid who's never seen a major league curve ball.'

"Uh-huh."

"You stood right up to it. So Buster tried something else."

"Uh-huh. A fastball, low and outside. And then a high fastball."

"Yes," Cal said with a grin, "and about the time the high fastball was leaving the infield, still on the rise, headed for the seats in left field, the first line was being written in the book on Ted Bell."

Ted's breakfast arrived—two eggs, scrambled, with bacon and toast, and orange juice and milk—and Cal's was right behind—poached egg on a muffin with coffee.

Ted ignored the breakfast a moment and nodded at Cal, waiting for him to continue.

"Everyone knows now that a fastball right down the middle, a little on the high side, can be a fatal pitch when Ted Bell is in the batter's box."

"I see."

"You won't be getting too many more of those."

Ted frowned. "In other words," he said, "the home run wasn't all that much hot stuff, huh?"

Cal picked up his knife and fork and went to work on the poached egg and muffin. "Oh, I didn't say that. A home run off Buster Krump is a real home run, no question about it. But you got served your favorite pitch, a luxury that is usually denied to Eddie Patterson—and Lou Mills."

Ted gave the man a sharp glance at the mention of Lou Mills. He started to speak.

"Better eat," Cal said, "before it gets cold."

When Ted walked into the dressing room, one by one the players turned and looked at him.

At first Ted thought they were staring at his new clothes— the maroon-and-white checked sport jacket, the dark gray shirt open at the collar, the gray slacks, the alligator shoes.

He started to smile, maybe even wave, to acknowledge the fact that they were noticing. But no, it was something else. Nobody smiled, nobody spoke. They just watched.

Puzzled, Ted nodded slightly and walked toward his stall. He felt their eyes follow him.

What was wrong?

He slipped off his sport jacket and hung it up, then began unbuttoning his shirt.

"If you want to play third base regularly, kid, you'd better pack your bags, head for Memphis, and set your sights on Omaha," said a voice behind him.

Ted turned. He stared into the face of Lou Mills.

"The old man ain't dead yet," Mills said.

"Huh?"

Mills turned his back on Ted without another word and walked away.

Everyone was looking at Ted.

From Ted's right, Eddie Patterson spoke in a low growl, "You've got a big mouth, kid, and you'd better be careful, or something is going to shut it for you."

Ted looked at Patterson. The big first baseman's naked stomach protruded above the belt of the athletic supporter, looming even larger than it had appeared in uniform. Ted suddenly realized what had happened. But . . . how? And what had Henry Jerome of the *Tulsa World* written?

"I—" He stopped. Nobody was looking at him now. They had all turned away.

Ted turned back to his stall. He felt his face flushing red. He'd never dreamed the sportswriter would make it sound like Ted thought Lou Mills was over the hill, finished. But apparently he had. Nor had Ted dreamed that Henry Jerome would quote him about the fat stomachs of the Kansas City Royals. But apparently he had.

But wait. No matter what he had written, how did the Royals know about it? The hotel newsstand didn't have the *Tulsa World*. And even if it did, how could everyone know so soon? The *Tulsa World* was a morning newspaper, so the story could not possibly appear before to-morrow morning. Ted frowned in puzzlement.

He finished unbuttoning his shirt, keeping his eyes straight ahead, fixed on the large number five on the back of the shirt hanging in the stall. Then he stopped. He turned to his right. Brian Stevens was pulling on his uniform shirt. He was looking straight ahead, paying no attention to Ted.

"What's happpened?" Ted asked in a low voice.

Brian looked at Ted, then glanced around quickly. "The AP reporter was in a few minutes ago with a copy of a story on the wire out of Tulsa," he said.

"Oh. And—"

Brian rolled his eyes toward the ceiling. "Did you really say those things?" he asked.

CHAPTER

5

Feeling very much alone, Ted sat on the bench for the second straight night. He watched the Royals beat the White Sox 4–3 on—of all things—Lou Mills's two-run homer in the seventh inning.

Nobody said anything more about Ted's quotes in the AP story out of Tulsa.

Once, in the idle period between the end of batting practice and the start of the game, when the grounds-keeper was making his final sweep of the infield dirt, Ted caught Hank Quincy watching him. Then Quincy started walking toward him in his bandy-legged way. Ted was sure the manager was coming over to scold him, right there on the edge of the dugout, in full view and hearing of everyone. But Quincy walked past Ted and stepped down into the dugout, taking his station at the end, ready for the game to start.

In the early innings Ted got the feeling his teammates

were shunning him. Seated at the opposite end of the dugout from where Hank Quincy had perched himself, Ted felt that the players strung out between him and the manager were a mile away. He might as well have been somewhere in the grandstand, or even outside the ball park. Players taking the field and returning to the dugout, or going up to the plate, never looked at him, never spoke to him.

Even Brian Stevens seemed to be ignoring Ted. In their room at the Hyatt Regency Hotel the night before, Brian had chattered easily about everything from hotels to Hank Quincy, from Ernie Rome to rainy-day pastimes. He had not mentioned his roommate's home run, which puzzled Ted. But he had been cheerful and open in clueing Ted in on the ropes with the Royals.

But now, during the game, the second baseman went about his business with eyes straight ahead, never glancing in Ted's direction. When Brian was called out on strikes in the fourth inning, he responded to Ted's call of consolation—"Tough, tough"—with only a curt nod, his eyes still straight ahead, away from Ted, as he took his seat on the bench.

Freddie Hanover had been one of the players reaching out and slapping Ted's hand when he returned to the dugout after powering Buster Krump's fastball over the left field wall the night before. But now Freddie sat far away from Ted, down the bench, and acted like the rookie did not exist.

Then Ted began to notice that the players treated each other—their teammates of years' standing—the same way they were treating the newcomer who had offended Lou Mills and Eddie Patterson.

The night before, when there was no cheering, no shouts of encouragement, just a silent addressing of the chores at hand, Ted attributed the mood to the shellacking the White Sox were dealing out to them.

But tonight, heading for a victory, they trudged to and from the field, to and from the plate, with the same dullness of the night before, silently and with eyes straight ahead.

Even when they got a run in the fourth—an Eddie Patterson double to deep right center that brought Mike Bedford racing home from first base—noboby came to life. Mike Bedford crossed home plate with all the excitement of a bricklayer putting another one in place. Eddie Patterson pulled up puffing at second base with his teammates in the dugout looking like they wanted to yawn. A couple of players sat forward to watch, but nothing more.

They were so businesslike, so mechanical—no cheers, no laughs, no frowns. The night before, taking a pasting from Buster Krump, nobody had seemed bothered. Now, with a chance to win, nobody seemed excited.

No, Ted decided, the Royals weren't shunning him any more than they were shunning each other.

The whole scene was new to Ted. He was used to cheering and moaning and laughing and frowning, because the game mattered.

He shrugged his shoulders and settled back on the bench, arms folded across his chest, cap tilted low over his eyes, and resolved not to worry. Maybe this was just the way major league players acted.

So Ted sat, unmoving, staring straight ahead, even at the moment of Lou Mills's game-winning home run, until the last out. Then he showered and dressed and climbed aboard the bus to the hotel.

Four days and three games later, slouched back on the bench in Seattle, watching the Royals play the Mariners, the idea came to Ted.

The precise moment was the top of the sixth inning—one out; Joe Randolph, the center fielder, at bat; two balls and one strike; the score 4–2 in favor of the Mariners.

The idea was so obvious, so simple, so logical—so right—that it brought Ted out of his slouching position. He sat up, straightened himself, and leaned forward, elbows on his knees. He marveled that the idea was so late in coming.

He watched Joe Randolph foul one off and then take a called third strike. He turned and glanced at Quincy, perched at the end of the dugout. Quincy didn't blink as

Joe let the third strike whistle past him, and Freddie Hanover marched toward the plate.

Ted needed to have a talk with Hank Quincy.

It was as simple as that. The time had come. Ted had ridden the bench for five games. He had not complained. But five games was enough. He could not prove himself while sitting on the bench. He could do that only on the field, playing third base and going to bat. Surely Hank Quincy could see that. If Ted batted and fielded better than Lou Mills—and he was sure he could—the Royals and Hank Quincy would be the beneficiaries of having Ted in the lineup. All that Ted needed was a chance. Surely Hank Quincy could see that. He would make Hank Quincy see it.

Ted leaned back again, pleased with the idea, as Freddie Hanover slapped a looping single over the third baseman's head into left field.

Ted always had had success in talking things out with adults, beginning with his parents. He had learned early that they would listen to reason. He thought things out before bringing them up for discussion. He discarded as harebrained the ideas that left questions unanswered, arguments lost in his own mind. And he discovered, as time passed, that his parents had more and more confidence in him. He nearly always got what he asked for, such as the chance to play baseball instead of going to Oklahoma State University. He'd had the same success with Coach Greene in three years of playing with the varsity baseball team—and even with Miss Cornelius when he was having trouble with algebra. Ted Bell knew how to handle adults in authority. And that included Hank Quincy.

On the field, Freddie Hanover was dancing off first base, trying to distract the pitcher, and Bomba Wright, at the end of the Royals' batting order, was stepping into the batter's box.

Ted glanced at Quincy. The manager had sent Ted to the plate for Bomba, the Royals' weakest hitter, on that first night with the Royals back in Chicago. Maybe now, with the Royals needing some runs, he would turn to Ted again. Bill Dickson, the backup catcher, could finish the game behind the plate. But Quincy wasn't even looking at Ted. He was staring idly at Bomba, now tapping his cleats with the bat.

Ted leaned back and pondered the best time to make his approach to Hank Quincy. Timing was important, whether making a pitch to his parents or to Miss Cornelius in algebra class—or to Hank Quincy. So far, this was a losing ball game for the Royals. Perhaps not the most propitious prelude to a conversation with the manager. But then again, maybe a losing game offered the best climate for discussing a possible change in the lineup. Maybe Hank Quincy would be more receptive to a change in the lineup and a chance for Ted, as he searched for methods to convert today's losing ways into tomorrow's winning ones.

But no, Hank Quincy always seemed to be sour and grouchy coming out of his meeting with the reporters after a game, win or lose. Even in victory he always had seen enough wrong to spoil his day. He was even grumpier after a loss. Ted had seen it four times. It was certain to be the same on this night, win or lose.

Ted nodded to himself slightly. The best time to talk to Quincy was before a game. And tomorrow would be soon enough.

At the plate, Bomba poked a feeble grounder through the box. The shortstop raced across, scooped it up, and touched second base. One down. He crossed the bag, eluding Freddie's slide, and fired the ball to first base. Two down. A double play and the side retired, a chance for a scoring rally lost.

Ted glanced at the scowling face of the manager at the end of the dugout. He knew that Hank Quincy was going to be a tougher customer for discussion than his parents or Coach Greene, for sure, and probably even tougher than Miss Cornelius. But he could do it.

The game ended without any more scoring, a 4–2 triumph for the Mariners over the Royals.

CHAPTER

B y the time Ted walked into the dressing room the next day, his world was not so simple.

It all had seemed so pat, so set, the night before as he sat on the bench in the dugout—talk to Hank Quincy, just as he had always talked to his parents, to Coach Greene, to Miss Cornelius.

What did he have to lose? Nothing.

What did he have to gain? Plenty. He might talk himself into a chance to play, to field and hit, to show what he could do. At the least, he would make the point with Quincy that he wanted to play, not just sit on the bench and draw his paycheck. Surely Hank Quincy ought to appreciate a player wanting to contribute.

But now, after the words of Brian Stevens in their hotel room the night before, Ted was less certain.

"Has Quincy said anything to you about playing regularly?"

Brian was sprawled in a chair with one leg looped over its arm.

Ted, in his pajamas, was in the bathroom rinsing his mouth after brushing his teeth. The question startled him, and he straightened up and looked at himself in the mirror. Was Brian Stevens able to read his mind? Did he know that Ted planned to talk to Quincy the next day? Surely not. Ted spit, wiped his mouth with a towel, and walked into the bedroom.

"No," he said. He wondered what prompted the question. So he asked, "Why?"

Brian shrugged and looked out the window at the city's light. "Just curious. Just wondering." Then he looked back at Ted. "Nothing from Quincy at all, huh?"

Ted frowned. "What are you getting at?"

"When you came up—joined the team in Chicago—did you think Quincy was going to slip you right into the lineup? I mean, did you expect to become a regular right away?"

Ted turned the small desk chair and dropped into it, facing Brian. "Well, yes, I guess—"

"But there'd been no promises, huh?"

"No," Ted said slowly. "No promises." Just his own assumption—an error, it seemed—that the Royals, having signed him and assigned him to the parent club, would play him.

"Lou Mills is pretty well set, pretty solid, at third base,"

Brian said, as if talking to himself. Then he looked at Ted. "He's slipped a little in the last couple of years. He's a little slower in the field, a little slower bringing the bat around, but he seems pretty solid at third base, don't you think?"

Ted studied Brian. He asked again, "What are you getting at?"

Brian shrugged and gave a tight little smile. "Well, I may as well come right out and ask you."

"Ask me what?"

"You haven't heard any talk, have you, about Quincy putting you in at second base?"

"Second base? I'm a third baseman."

"So? Babe Ruth was a pitcher who became a right fielder. People change positions. A decision about where to play you that was made three or four years ago by a high-school coach isn't something etched in stone. It's not a lifetime commitment, you know."

Ted rubbed his jaw. "I never thought about that." He looked at his roommate and wondered if the threat to Brian's job—real or imagined—explained his coolness toward Ted in the dugout. "Have your heard something about it?"

"There's been some talk. I was wondering if there was anything to it."

"I guess you were."

"Well?"

"No, Quincy's never mentioned second base—or anything else, including third base, for that matter."

Brian nodded. "Just wondering."

Ted said nothing for a moment. He let the new idea—new to him, at least—settle in his mind. It never had occurred to him. But it might be a possibility. He knew that Pete Rose had played all over the field. People did change positions.

"Quincy sure could use your bat in the lineup," Brian said. His tone of voice almost put a question mark at the end of the sentence.

"He doesn't act much like it. Why, just tonight, with Freddie on first and Bomba going up there and hitting into a double play . . ."

"Yeah, I know. I thought he was going to send you up."

For a moment Ted considered confiding to Brian that he was going to talk with Quincy about getting a chance to play. But Brian's worries about holding on to his second base job stopped him. What if Quincy did have second base in mind for Ted? Quincy may well have decided that Ted's bat wasn't worth benching the legendary Lou Mills but was surely a better bat than the light hitting of Brian Stevens. As for fielding, if Ted Bell could grab 'em at third base, he could grab 'em at second base. Brian Stevens, his roommate, might be Ted's rival, not Lou

Mills. So Ted decided against telling Brian of his plan to talk with Quincy.

"But he didn't send me up to hit for Bomba," Ted said finally.

Brian let the remark go by without comment. "Everybody's been a little worried," he said.

"Worried? About what?"

Brian grinned. "You."

"Really?" Ted had arrived thinking that Lou Mills was going to have to make plans. So Lou Mills might be worried. But anyone else? He asked, "Why?"

Brian lifted his leg off the arm of the chair and put his foot on the floor, leaning forward. "Well, a rookie shows up with a big reputation. The rookie is a third baseman. But our present third baseman is great. So where is the rookie going to play? Probably not third base. So how about second base, or left field, or whatever?" He paused. "They've signed you and they've brought you up. Everybody figures they've got to play you."

"Did you say left field?"

Brian chuckled. "Mike Bedford was asking if anyone had heard anything about you playing left field. He's not been playing well, you know, and a guy gets sort of paranoid."

"The outfield," Ted said in disbelief.

"Anything's possible."

"I don't think that is. Anyway, I'm still on the bench—nowhere. I don't even pinch-hit for Bomba."

"It'll change," Brian said, leaning back.

Ted shrugged. "I don't think Quincy likes me."

Brian laughed. "Hank Quincy doesn't like anyone."

Later, in bed, with the lights out, Ted stared into the darkness and let Brian's suggestion that Quincy might be toying with the idea of playing him at second base race through his mind. Should he postpone talking to the manager? Maybe Quincy was on the brink of making a move. Ted's plea might serve only to irritate him. Or should he perhaps go ahead with his sales pitch—and include the possibility of second base? No, no. He couldn't go after Brian's job. But then, what was so different about going after Brian's job? He wanted to go after Lou Mills's. So why not Brian's? But no, he would not mention second base to Quincy. If Quincy ordered it on his own initiative, okay. There was nothing to be done. But Ted could never bring himself to make the suggestion.

But then again . . .

The questions whirled through Ted's mind until he finally dropped off to sleep.

There were five players in the dressing room when Ted walked in. Lou Mills and Eddie Patterson were in the whirlpool room. Mike Bedford was in the lounge reading *The Wall Street Journal*. Harold Johnson was autographing balls. Bomba Wright was sitting on a stool reading a letter.

Ernie Rome gave Ted a quizzical look. Ted didn't need the whirlpool treatment. He wasn't carrying a copy of *The Wall Street Journal*. Nobody cared if he autographed the balls. He did not receive fan letters. So why was Ted Bell an hour early?

Ted walked across the dressing room to the short hallway leading to Hank Quincy's office. He nodded when Harold Johnson plunked a signed ball back into the box and looked up. He waved through the door to the lounge when Mike Bedford glanced up over *The Wall Street Journal*. He saw Lou Mills and Eddie Patterson looking at him from the whirlpool room when he passed the door.

Quincy was in his office, seated at his desk. He was leaning back, his hands clasped behind his neck and his feet up on the desk, staring into space.

Ted stopped in the doorway. "May I see you a minute?"

Quincy, far from startled out of his reverie, seemed almost to have been expecting Ted. He turned his head slightly and looked at Ted. "What is it?"

Ted waited a moment for Quincy to invite him in. The question always drew an invitation from Coach Greene. But Quincy simply stared. Ted hesitated, then stepped through the door and approached a chair near Quincy's desk.

Quincy, unmoving, watched Ted cross the office. The

manager looked like he was smelling something unpleasant. His expression seemed to tell Ted he was a loser before he began. Did Hank Quincy know what Ted was planning to say? It seemed so, and the thought put a frown on Ted's face. For a brief moment he regretted the whole idea. The night before, sitting on the bench in the dugout, the idea had seemed so good, so right. But now Ted wanted to mumble, "Nothing, nothing at all," and flee the room, escaping Hank Quincy's icy gaze. But instead he kept moving toward the chair. He erased the frown from his face and even managed a small smile. He sat down on the chair.

"What is it?" Quincy asked again.

"I wanted to talk. . . ." Ted's well-rehearsed script eluded him under Quincy's glare.

"Talk? Talk about what?"

Ted took a deep breath. "I haven't played yet—well, just once as a pinch hitter—and I think that if I had the chance . . ."

Quincy watched without expression, no help at all.

"If I had a chance to show you what I can do . . ." Ted said, leaving the sentence unfinished. Quincy continued to watch without expression. "I figured when I signed and was going to join the club, I would have a chance to play—to show what I can do. But all I'm doing is sitting on the bench, and . . ."

Ted let the words trail off when Quincy abruptly swung

his feet off the desk and turned in his chair to face Ted. He placed his hands, palms down, flat on the desk. He leaned forward. He was going to nail Ted. Ted could see it coming. He waited.

"Were you promised anything?"

Ted involuntarily shook his head. Then he asked, "You mean, when I signed?"

"Then, or before, or after? Were you promised anything?"

"Well, that I was going to join the club."

"And you have done that."

"But I just assumed . . ."

"Assumed what?"

Ted took another deep breath. This wasn't the way things usually went with his parents, or Coach Greene, or Miss Cornelius. "I assumed that I was going to get a chance to play, to show you what I can do."

Quincy leaned back in the chair. He did not look angry. He certainly did not look amused or interested. He looked bored. Maybe, Ted now thought with some regret, every rookie looking for his chance had made a similar pitch to Quincy for more than ten years and the manager was weary of listening. Ted waited.

"Look, kid," Quincy said, his scratchy voice possessing a conversational tone, "this isn't Broken Bow High School, or wherever you came from. This is major league baseball. I'm not some underpaid, dedicated coach assigned to assist you in your physical and character development. I'm the manager of the Kansas City Royals. My job is to win baseball games. When I think that having you in the lineup will help win games, then I'll put you in the lineup. Until then, don't bother me. You're just wasting your breath and my time."

He said it all in such a matter-of-fact way that it wasn't until he had finished that Ted began to feel a flash of anger. Hank Quincy had not just turned him down, he had cut him off. He had not just refused to consider Ted's plea, he had refused even to hear it. Ted knew that his anger showed in his face, and he knew that Quincy recognized the anger. Then he realized that Quincy had intended to anger him or, perhaps, simply did not care. Either way, the experience was a new one for Ted Bell. Nobody in Genoa ever had spoken to him that way.

Quincy sat silently, waiting for Ted.

Ted swallowed and fought back the feeling of anger. "I can win games for you," he said finally, feeling a bit foolish.

"I'll be the judge of that," Quincy replied. He paused and looked Ted up and down—the new sport shirt and blazer, the new slacks, and, for what seemed like a full minute, the alligator shoes—and said, "Look, you're being paid, aren't you?"

"Yes."

"Then shut up and try to grow up."

Ted felt his face flush red. He started to say, "I want to be traded, I'll never play for you." But he said nothing. His mouth felt dry. He managed to nod and got to his feet. He thought: How dumb can the manager of a major league baseball team be? But he said nothing. He turned and somehow walked out of the office.

CHAPTER

The open date before the first game of the home stand against Minnesota was no bonus for Ted. If sitting on the bench was bad, sitting around a hotel room was worse. Even walking the streets of strange cities taking in the sights was rapidly becoming a bore. Besides, he already had walked the streets of Kansas City.

Ted wanted to play baseball. He wanted to play every day. He would have been happy with doubleheaders every day. Ever since the day his father had brought home a baseball, a bat, and a glove, back when Ted was six years old, all he ever had wanted to do was throw and catch and bat a baseball.

But here he was, doing nothing but sitting—on a bench in a dugout, or in a seat on an airplane, or on the edge of a bed in a hotel room.

More and more, Ted found himself wondering about Charleston, Jacksonville, Omaha—the minor leagues—

where he might have been able to bat and spear line drives and scoop up grounders every day. Maybe he had made a mistake in demanding a place on the Royals' roster as part of the price of signing.

And here in Kansas City, the home base of the Royals, Ted didn't have even the occasional company of a roommate. Brian maintained an apartment in Kansas City. He did not need a hotel room shared with Ted. And Brian had a girlfriend to spend his time with. He did not need the company of Ted Bell.

The sky outside the hotel room window was heavy with dark clouds. Ted got up from the bed and walked to the window, staring out at the clouds. If it was going to rain, he preferred it on this free day. Better that than on a game day.

The jangle of the telephone on the bedside table startled Ted. He knew no one outside the Royals in Kansas City. And most of them, like Brian, maintained a home in the city. They had family and friends here. They had no reason to call Ted Bell, a rookie newcomer. Ted walked across the room toward the ringing telephone, deciding that the caller was his father, who would know from the schedule that this was a free day.

He picked up the telephone. "Hello."

"Ted, this is Cal."

"Oh, hi, Cal," Ted said. "What can I do for you?"

"It's a free day, and I thought you might like to come

over and help Myrna and me grill some steaks. It'll beat sitting around a hotel room watching the Angels win another one."

Ted glanced at the blank television screen. He hadn't even thought of tuning in the game. "I wasn't watching. Are they winning again?"

"It's six to one in the third," Cal said. "They chased Marty Marino with four runs in the first, and now they're working over Roy Dollarway."

Ted grinned. That was a pitcher's view of a baseball game—not who was doing the hitting but who was pitching and giving up the runs.

"I can pick you up at the hotel," Cal continued. "No problem at all. What do you say?"

"Sounds great."

"So you batted .680," Cal said. "That's just about incredible, even against high school pitchers."

Ted and Cal were seated on folding chairs on the redwood deck at the rear of the Hanleys' yellow brick house in a Kansas City suburb. Beyond the deck, a carpet of grass was dotted with well-tended flower beds in full bloom—doubtless the work of a baseball widow with time on her hands while her husband traveled with the team. The Hanleys had bought the house ten years earlier when they decided that Kansas City was home, no matter where Cal's career might take him. As it turned out, his career had taken him no place, except for a regular paycheck from the Royals for coaching and making an occasional appearance in relief. Ted and Cal were sipping iced tea from tall glasses, and off to the left, at the edge of the deck, smoke was wafting up from the burning charcoal in a large red kettle grill. The dark rain clouds had blown over, and the early evening sky was a light blue.

"I never had any trouble hitting," Ted said. "It always just seemed to come naturally."

"I've always admired hitters," Cal said.

"That's a funny thing for a pitcher to say."

Cal smiled and shrugged slightly. "Hitting is the most difficult feat in all of sports, bar none."

"Really?" Ted said. He never had thought of hitting as difficult. "I always thought that pitching—"

"Oh, no. Pitching is just throwing. People have been throwing something—rocks at saber-toothed tigers, for example—as long as they've been around. It's probably built in the genes by this time. Throwing is a natural function. But hitting, that's another matter. Think of what a hitter has to do."

Ted grinned. "Just swing."

"No, no. Think about it. A hitter has to hit one round object, the ball, with another round object, the bat. There's nothing like it in any other sport. Passing a football— that's just throwing. Scoring a field goal in basketball— that's just throwing, with a greater demand for accuracy.

In golf you're at least hitting the round object, the ball, with a flat surface. No, think about it. Soccer, tennis, even jai alai—there's nothing in any of them demanding the skill that's necessary to hit a round object with another round object—and do it successfully. No, I admire hitters. Always have."

"I never thought of it that way." Ted chuckled slightly and added, "And now that I've finally found out how difficult it is, I probably won't be able to do it anymore."

"Oh, yes, you will. Anyone who can pound Buster Krump's fastball out of the park is a hitter. You're a hitter."

Ted took a sip of the iced tea. Then he grinned at Cal. "At least until they've finished writing the book on me, huh?"

Cal shook his head. "I've got a feeling that writing the book on you is going to give the pitchers only temporary comfort. You'll hit them, no matter what. I've watched you in practice. Every movement—perfect."

"Then why—"

The glass door to their right slid open, and Myrna Hanley emerged with a platter of T-bone steaks. "Isn't the fire ready yet?"

"Sure," Cal said. He got to his feet and took the platter from his wife. "Have a seat. I'll put them on."

Myrna sat in the chair vacated by Cal and turned to

Ted. "So you're from Oklahoma. I have a brother living in Oklahoma City."

At the grill, Cal was putting the steaks on the fire.

After dinner Ted and Cal helped Myrna clear away the dishes and then watched the final inning of the Angels' victory on television.

"Good team—strong pitching," Cal said as he flicked off the television set and they moved toward the sliding glass doors to return to the deck. "We'll be outside," he called to his wife.

Myrna poked her head out of the kitchen door. "While you two discuss the merits of swinging on a two-and-oh pitch, I'm going to catch up on some letter writing."

Cal grinned at her, and he and Ted stepped through the door, slid it shut behind them, and took seats.

Ted studied Cal for a moment in the dim glow of the light from inside the house. Cal Hanley was an old man—by baseball standards. He was probably in his early forties, Ted guessed. He was about the same age as Ted's father, who was forty-two. Mr. Bell was considered a young man to have the job he held, president of Genoa Junior College. But Cal Hanley was an old man in baseball. His best years were behind him, not out front in the future. He was almost finished. The only question now was which year was to be his last. When would he throw his last strike? When would he pull on a uniform for the last time?

"You're finding out that there's a lot of politics in baseball," Cal said.

The statement surprised Ted. Politics in baseball? No, baseball was just hitting and pitching and fielding. "What do you mean?" he asked.

"You're on the squad—up here with the Royals instead of in the minors—because of orders from the front office, and you're riding the bench because of a decision by Hank Quincy," Cal said. "The two of them, the front office and Quincy, are at loggerheads over the questions of Ted Bell and Lou Mills."

Ted leaned forward. He was interested. "I don't follow you," he said.

Cal took a deep breath and sighed. "Lou Mills was— no, let me correct that, still is—one of the greatest third basemen who ever played the game. But he's nearing the end of the line. Age is catching up with him. All the signs are there. He's slowing down, by a fraction of a second, a half step. But he *is* slowing down."

Cal paused, as if weighing a thought, perhaps a thought about the approaching end of his own career in the game that had been his life.

"Everybody knows it, of course, including Hank Quincy and Lou Mills, but nobody says anything about it—except you."

A slight grin on Cal's face was visible in the faint light on the deck.

Ted started to speak, but he didn't know what to say.

It didn't matter. Cal waved him into silence and continued.

"And along comes a young third baseman named Ted Bell. The smart boys who run the ball club figured that a Ted Bell doesn't come along every year. Here was the chance to snag Lou Mills's successor. So they agreed to put Ted Bell on the roster right away, as he demanded—without spending a year or so in the minors—and they signed him. They figured they could always trade Lou Mills to a team that needed a great third baseman with only a few years left. It'd be a team that had not yet found their Ted Bell. Do you see?"

"I think so. But—"

"But there was Hank Quincy," Cal interrupted. "Quincy is under a lot of heat this year. He's won four pennants and two World Series along the way, but not in a while. That makes it tough for him in a sport where four years ago—or even last year—doesn't matter worth a plugged nickel. The only thing that matters in baseball is this year. The front office wants a pennant, maybe a World Series flag, and Quincy is going to deliver or he's going to go."

"Uh-huh."

"The front office signed you and wants to trade Lou

while they can still get something for him—all with an eye to the future. And it makes sense. But Quincy can't afford to worry about the future. If he doesn't win the flag this year, there won't be any future for him. And he's more comfortable with the tried-and-true Lou Mills than with a rookie who just arrived from an Oklahoma high school. The front office, demanding that Quincy deliver, has got to let Quincy do it his way. See?"

"But then what happens?"

Cal grinned slightly again. "If Quincy wins, you'll probably be on your way to the minors next year to wait out the honorable retirement of Lou Mills. Quincy will have been proved right." He paused. "If Quincy loses, he'll get the boot—no doubt about it—and the smart boys running the club will put Lou Mills on the trading block and you'll probably have yourself a job—or at least a shot at a job—with a new manager."

Ted frowned. Then he leaned back in the chair, the frown still in place. "If you're right," he said slowly, "I haven't even got a chance of winning the job this year on my own ability."

"Probably not," Cal said. "But sometimes things happen. Who knows?"

"Yeah, I guess," Ted said. "Who knows?"

CHAPTER

Cal Hanley had said, "Sometimes things happen. Who knows?"

And now, ten games later, in the second of a three-game series against the Oakland A's, something had. Lou Mills, after fighting a head cold for four days, finally had succumbed. He had taken to his bed in the hotel. Ted Bell was on the field at third base taking the pregame fielding warm-up with the Royals. He was going to start at third base.

The ten games—against the Twins, the A's, the Angels, then the A's again—had dragged by for Ted. His role had been to sit on the bench, feet up, arms folded across his chest, watching Lou Mills play third base and step up to the plate and bat.

Watching, Ted had decided that Cal Hanley was right about Lou Mills slowing down. At the plate, Mills was a fraction of a second late in starting his swing. The time was widening between the moment his eyes and brain told him to swing and his body reacted—only slightly but widening nevertheless.

The opposing pitchers had noticed, and Mills was getting more than his share of blazing fastballs.

When Mills hit, he seemed almost to pause for a breath before breaking into a sprint for first base—a pause of only a flicker of a second but enough to make a difference.

In the field he hesitated—again, for only the briefest of moments, but nevertheless a hesitation—before diving for a line drive or charging forward on a grounder.

Time and again, Ted caught himself shaking his head, certain beyond a doubt that he could have run out the infield hit that Mills missed by a half step, or speared the line drive that Mills only knocked down, or thrown out the bunter who outran Mills's throw. Ted was so sure, so very sure, every time.

Was Hank Quincy blind?

But the manager, with good eyesight or poor, seldom even glanced in Ted's direction. And he never, not once, showed disappointment at a late throw or a slow start to first base by Lou Mills. He scowled, to be sure, but Hank Quincy always scowled at everyone.

It seemed that every time Ted decided that now, now surely, Hank Quincy would change his mind, Lou Mills came through. He hit three home runs in the ten games during which Ted rode the bench. Once he doubled home the winning run for Kansas City in the ninth. And in the field it seemed that every time Ted finished shaking his head at what he considered to be a flawed play, Mills reached back into his greatness to pull off a spectacular play.

Ted could not help noticing that the other players were pulling for Mills. To the older players Mills was a long-time friend whose greater days they remembered. Eddie Patterson, while not one to cheer anything, always managed to catch Mills's eye and give a curt nod of approval when the veteran third baseman made a good play. Among the younger players, such as Brian Stevens, and, yes, Ted Bell, too, Lou Mills was an idol, a hero, a legend of their boyhood sandlot days, now in their presence as a teammate. They maintained a quiet and respectful distance from him, as if awestruck by the person of the great third baseman. Ted understood. He knew he was trying to replace—or rather, displace—a legend. But the time had come. Ted was sure of it.

Was Hank Quincy blind?

"No, Hank Quincy is not blind," Cal Hanley had told Ted at lunch one day in Los Angeles. "But he's conservative. All baseball men are. They like the status quo. They hate and fear change and innovation. They're comfortable with the tried-and-true." And with a smile he added, "Why, if baseball men had been running the world when the wheel was invented, we'd still be weighing all the implications before deciding what to do with it."

Ted managed a grin despite his frustration.

Brian had not mentioned again the threat of Quincy putting Ted at second base. Ted never mentioned it, either. If Hank Quincy was too conservative to try Ted at third base—his real position—he surely wasn't about to start switching positions. Maybe Brian had come to the same conclusion.

As for Lou Mills, he went about his work as if Ted Bell did not exist. Ted might as well have been a batboy. The third baseman never acknowledged Ted's presence with as much as a nod. Maybe he was still thinking about Ted's words in the interview with the sportswriter at the *Tulsa World*. Maybe he still remembered Ted's remarks in the locker room when they first met. Or maybe he simply did not think that Ted Bell—a kid, a rookie— mattered enough to warrant a word or a nod. Eddie Patterson acted the same, and the other players seemed to be following their lead. They never extended them- selves to Ted in a friendly way. Ted shrugged at their behavior. It didn't matter. He was bound to get his chance, and that was when things would matter.

In the pregame infield warm-up, Ted felt good. The Kansas City night was clear and cool. The dull *thunk* of the ball smacking into the pocket of his glove sounded good. Massaging the ball in the pocket with his right hand to take a grip for the throw brought back the thrill of a hundred other games, a thousand other throws to first base. Rifling the ball into Eddie Patterson's huge glove felt good. Ted was going to play after three weeks of sitting on the bench watching Lou Mills.

In the batter's cage he sprayed line drives to right field, center field, left field. The pitches coming at him, the stitches clearly visible to his sharp eye, gave him a thrill. His smooth swing of the bat, wrists snapping at the instant of contact with the ball, felt good. The sharp, cracking sound of bat meeting ball was exhilarating. He was going to be batting in a game for the first time in twenty-one days. He could not remember a summer in his life when three weeks had passed without playing in a baseball game. But he was going to play tonight.

Cal Hanley, walking past the batting cage, winked at Ted. The rookie grinned back and slapped the next pitch into deep left center field.

Ted was ready to play. But even more, he was ready for his chance. He kept recalling the story of Lou Gehrig, an untried rookie with the Yankees, stepping in one day for an ailing Wally Pipp. Pipp never got the job back. Gehrig won it away from him in one game. The story always had fascinated Ted. It was a measure of the legendary first baseman's natural ability. But of late, the story fascinated him for another reason. He was planning to duplicate the feat. On this clear June night in Kansas City, Lou Mills, who was nursing a head cold in a downtown hotel, was going to lose his third base job with the Royals to Ted Bell.

Ted wondered if Hank Quincy knew the Lou Gehrig story. Probably so. Baseball people, more than the people in other sports, had a sense of the history of their game. They knew about the great players of the past. They relished the retelling of the great moments. Baseball players were fans of their own game. So, sure, Hank Quincy knew the Lou Gehrig story.

But Quincy hadn't acted like the story was in his mind when he told Ted he was going to play. There was not the slightest indication that the crusty old manager knew he was facing a historic moment. He simply walked over to Ted's stall and stated matter-of-factly, "Mills is down with the cold. It'll be you tonight." He might have been announcing a cloudy sky. He just said the words, turned, and walked away without waiting for an answer.

The sudden announcement had come as a surprise to Ted. He knew, as everyone did, that a head cold was bothering Mills. The third baseman had sneezed and coughed his way through the previous night's game. But Ted had not expected it to sideline Mills. Ted had played plenty of times with a sore throat and a stuffy nose.

Ted had turned at the sound of Quincy's voice and, speaking to the manager's departing back, said, "O-*kay!*"

When he turned back to his stall, a smile on his face, Brian Stevens leaned in toward him. "Okay, kid," he said with a smile, "you're on." The word *kid* sounded funny coming from Brian, who could not have been more than three years older than Ted.

"You bet!" Ted replied.

When Ted went into his crouch at third base for the first time, facing the first Oakland batter, he heard Freddie Hanover calling to him. He turned. "In a little, in a little," the shortstop said, waving his right hand to gesture Ted a step or two forward.

Ted instinctively bristled at being told how to play his position. It had never happened to him before. And worse yet, he wasn't just being told where to station himself. He was being waved into position. All of his teammates, the thousands of fans in the grandstands, and the people watching on television—maybe a million of them—were seeing that the rookie playing for Lou Mills had to be told where to position himself. Probably the announcer was pointing it out to his audience at this very moment. Ted felt a slight flush of embarrassment. He was not used to being embarrassed on a baseball field. For a moment he considered shaking off Freddie's directions and holding his ground. He knew how to play third base.

But Ted had to acknowledge that Freddie Hanover, a five-year veteran with the Royals, knew the tendencies of the hitters in the league—the pull hitters, the opposite-field hitters, the heavy hitters who slammed screaming line drives, the stick hitters who tried to poke grounders through holes in the infield.

Also, Freddie had a good line of sight to Bomba Wright's signals to the pitcher from behind the plate. He knew the name of the upcoming pitch and where it was supposed to go.

So Ted nodded at Freddie and moved forward two steps.

The leadoff batter, after watching a ball and a called strike, stroked a weak grounder to the shortstop. Freddie stepped to his right, scooped up the ball, and threw out the runner.

As the next batter stepped into the box Ted heard Freddie's voice again. "Back up and to your left, this way," he said. Ted gritted his teeth as he followed the shortstop's directions. At least he wasn't waving at him this time.

The batter swung on the first pitch and sent a scorching line drive, chest-high, straight for the place where Ted was standing. Ted threw up his glove and caught the rifle shot.

He turned and threw the ball across to Freddie.

Freddie caught the ball and smiled at Ted. "Okay?" he asked, obviously sensing Ted's resentment of the directions.

Ted nodded. "Yeah, okay," he said, managing a half smile.

The teams rocked along scoreless for three innings, with Ted lining out to the shortstop his first time at bat.

In the top of the fourth inning Ted was playing close to the line and deep against a right-handed hitter. The batter slammed a line drive, waist-high, between Ted and Freddie. The screamer had "base hit" written all over it.

Ted sprang to his left in a frantic dash the moment the ball left the bat. Then, with gloved hand extended, he left his feet in a desperate dive. He knocked the ball to the ground and landed in a heap next to it. Picking up the ball in his right hand, he scrambled to his knees and, from the kneeling position deep in the infield, fired the ball across to first base, beating the runner by a step.

Eddie Patterson's usually expressionless face gave way to a look of astonishment as he brought up his huge glove and took in the throw.

As Ted got to his feet, the roaring cheer of thirty thousand Kansas City fans rolled down and across the field.

Ted looked from Eddie Patterson to Freddie Hanover. The shortstop, his mouth agape, was standing with his arms dangling loosely at his sides, staring at Ted.

The cheers of the crowd turned to applause and continued as the next batter stepped to the plate.

Ted glanced at the Royals dugout. Hank Quincy was off his perch, standing, hands on hips, looking at Ted.

Ted heard Brian's voice from across the infield: "Hey, baby—okay!"

Ted nodded. The applause of the crowd continued. He finally touched the brim of his cap in acknowledgment and listened for Freddie's directions for the next batter.

In the home half of the sixth inning the Royals punched across three runs, one of them on Ted's long single to left center field, then coasted to a 3–1 triumph.

As Ted trooped through the tunnel to the locker room with the other players, he relived his role in the game. All in all, not bad, he decided. True, he got only one hit in four trips, but that one hit scored a run. His liner to the shortstop, if only a few feet to either side, would have gone for extra bases. His fly-out to deep left field would have been a home run in some parks. He shrugged off the would-have-beens. They did not count in the batting average. He had struck out on his other trip to the plate. Not even a would-have-been there. But all in all, not bad.

In the field he had handled five chances without error, one of them a spectacular play.

No, all in all, not bad.

But Hank Quincy announced to the reporters gathered in his office that he was confident Lou Mills would be sufficiently recovered from his head cold to resume his role at third base for the Royals the next night.

From there to the All-Star break—fourteen days with eleven games—Ted Bell sat on the bench and watched Lou Mills perform. He sat in the familiar position— slouched back, feet up, arms crossed over his chest, unmoving—and stared without expression from under the bill of his cap.

"I thought you'd won yourself a job when you threw out that runner from your knees," Cal Hanley told Ted.

"Well, Quincy didn't."

Cal grinned. "I'll bet that one play did more to cure Lou Mills's head cold than all the medicine they gave him. He probably experienced instant recovery when he saw what happened on his television screen."

"Anything I can do to help," Ted said with a weak grin.

"Quincy's hard to figure. Don't give up."

"Sure."

But it was a dejected Ted Bell who walked out of the ballpark in Baltimore, following a 2–0 Kansas City loss, to begin the break for the All-Star game. He caught a cab to the airport and boarded a flight to Dallas, the first leg of a trip home to Genoa for three days.

As a third baseman, he was going nowhere. And he was doing it with a team that was going nowhere. He was riding the bench, and the Royals were wallowing in sixth place in the American League West standings.

He wondered what he was going to tell his parents and friends in Genoa.

CHAPTER 9

For three of the Royals, Lou Mills among them, the All-Star Game meant a flight to San Francisco to play in the premiere game of the season, the best of the American League against the best of the National League.

But for Ted Bell and the others, the All-Star Game meant a three-day break in the grueling grind of the baseball season—a brief respite from the endless round of airplane rides, a change from the sights and sounds of strange cities, a chance to escape from the hotel rooms that somehow had all come to look alike.

It was a break, too, from the routine of going to ball parks, where some people played baseball but Ted Bell sat on a bench and watched.

Most of the players used this break for a trip home. Others went fishing, unbothered that they would miss seeing the game on television. A few headed for the beaches.

Ted had mixed feelings about going home for the All-Star break. Sure, it would be good to see his parents and friends, to sleep in his own room, to eat home-cooked meals again. But with his grand total of five at-bats and nine innings of play in the field to show for his thirty games in a Royals uniform, he dreaded facing the people back in Genoa. Ted Bell was not exactly returning home a conquering hero. He wasn't even returning as the Royals' third baseman. There were going to be questions.

The toughest questions were sure to come from his parents. If you're not playing regularly, what about college? If you're headed for the minor leagues next year, is that what you want? Why not college instead? Ted did not know the answers.

There were going to be other questions, too—from his former Genoa High teammates, his other friends, Coach Greene, even Doc Gaylord at the drugstore and Mr. Pappas at the cafe. And those who didn't ask questions, well, they were going to give him questioning looks.

Ted knew what he was heading for, and he knew he was not going to enjoy it.

On the overnight flight to Dallas he managed to doze off a couple of times but got no real sleep. The first dim grayness of dawn was on the eastern horizon when the plane touched down at Dallas. Ted stretched, rubbed his eyes, and waited in his seat while the plane taxied toward the terminal.

Next to him, a man in a rumpled business suit stirred, then brought himself upright and glanced out the window.

"We here?" he asked.

"Yep," Ted said.

Ted had not told his seatmate this time that he was the new third baseman for the Kansas City Royals.

And when he got up and left the plane, he walked past a smiling flight attendant who also had not been told that Ted Bell was the new third baseman for the Kansas City Royals.

"Have a nice day," the flight attendant said.

"Sure," Ted replied.

Ted walked through the terminal and found the gate for his connecting flight to Tulsa, where his parents would be meeting him. He had an hour to wait. He took a seat, then spotted a newspaper someone had left on a seat across from him. He walked over, picked up the paper, and returned to his seat. Around him, the few people in the waiting area were easy to separate into the all-night passengers making a plane change and the travelers starting out fresh after a night's sleep.

Ted leafed through the newspaper to the sports section

and found Lou Mills's face staring out of the page at him. This was going to be the third baseman's twelfth straight All-Star Game, and somebody had interviewed him. Ted laid the paper, unread, on the seat next to him, leaned back, and closed his eyes.

The late-morning sun was high and hot when he stepped off the plane in Tulsa and walked into the terminal, looking around for his parents.

"Ted!"

He heard his mother's voice and turned to see his parents coming toward him.

He hugged his mother and kissed her on the cheek, then shook his father's hand.

"Long flight?" his father asked.

"Yeah, long."

"You look tired," his mother said.

"I am."

During the ride to Genoa from the Tulsa airport, Mr. Bell, at the wheel, said, "I've gone ahead and enrolled you at Oklahoma State for the fall semester."

Ted, in the backseat, met his father's glance in the rearview mirror.

"Just in case," Mr. Bell added.

Ted nodded. "Okay."

After a moment his father said, "We thought we'd have

a cookout the night of the All-Star Game—you know, Coach Greene and some of your friends—and watch the game together. Okay with you?"

"Sounds good."

Ted leaned back in the seat, grateful that his father had let the subject of college drop for the moment. Ted was too weary to discuss the relative merits of sitting on the bench with the Royals as opposed to leaving the team for college. And he was too mixed up in his own mind.

The choice—to stay with the Royals, waiting and hoping, or to give up ever getting a chance—had been rolling around in his mind for two weeks. The choice had become very real to him on the night he'd played against the A's, while Lou Mills tended a head cold at the hotel. Ted had played well, at bat and in the field, only to learn that Hank Quincy had promptly announced he was sure Lou Mills would be ready to go again the next night. In that instant Ted saw a future he did not like—riding the bench, untried, to the end of the season, and then an assignment to some minor league club next season to begin the long climb back. The "Lou Gehrig Caper" had not worked for him. So now what?

Many good players had played away their careers without ever getting their big chance. Ted had read of several cases. He would not be the first. What if it happened to him? A lackluster career and then, at age forty or so, no job—and no college education. No, no, he knew he had to get a college education. He was only putting it off. But for what? A career on the bench? A career in the minor leagues?

If only Hank Quincy would give him a chance to show—

"We're home."

Mrs. Bell's voice from the front seat brought Ted up with a start.

"You went to sleep," his mother said.

"Yeah, I guess so."

Ted looked out the windows of the car. There was the house—red brick, white trim, wide front porch. There was the huge old oak tree where he and Louie Morris had built a tree house when they were in grade school. The car was parked in the driveway where he and his father had played catch with a baseball a thousand times. It was good to be home for a couple of days.

There was no avoiding the question as Ted ran into an old friend later that day.

"Hey, you're not playing much, are you?" Charlie Atkinson asked. Charlie had played center field on the Genoa High team and had a baseball scholarship to Tulsa University. He was on his lunch break as lifeguard at Lake Hobson. He and Ted were seated at a picnic table under a tree next to the refreshment stand. The beach around them and the shallow part of the lake were dotted with youngsters and parents. "I look at the Royals' box score every morning, and—"

"One game and one pinch-hit, that's all," Ted said.

He and Charlie had been close friends as well as teammates for three years. Coming from Charlie, the direct question did not bother Ted.

"What's the problem? I thought . . ." Charlie let his voice trail off. "Well, you know . . ."

Ted shrugged and managed a small grin. "Well, the manager seems to think their other third baseman is doing okay."

Charlie watched Ted for a moment. "You hit a homer your first time up," he said.

"Yep." The home run seemed a million years ago to Ted.

"We all cheered when we read about it," Charlie said. Then he smiled and added, "Except Archie McHenry."

Ted grinned. "Yeah, good ol' Archie." Archie McHenry was a pitcher—and a good one—who made no secret about resenting all the rave notices tumbling around Genoa High's sensational third baseman instead of their leading pitcher.

"But then, after that home run—well, nothing—and, well, what happened?"

"Back to the bench, that's all."

"Have your talked to the manager? What does he say?"

Ted frowned. He did not enjoy being reminded of his

conversation with Hank Quincy. "I tried to. But he's not much for talking."

"What are you going to do?"

"I don't know."

Later, in Pappas's Cafe, where a lot of the kids always gathered, Ted looked up to see Mr. Pappas grinning down on him.

"A home run the very first time at bat," he said. "We were all thrilled for you, and very proud."

Ted mumbled, "Thanks," and waited for the question, But why aren't you playing more?

But Mr. Pappas continued to smile and then walked away, not asking the direct question that Ted was sure he saw in the man's eyes.

In the late afternoon, when Ted knew that Coach Greene would be home from his summertime job coaching in the park district, Ted drove to his house near the high school. He knew his high school coach was going to want to hear every detail of his first month with the Royals.

But as they seated themselves in the wicker chairs on the front porch, Coach Greene's first question came as a surprise. "That story in the *Tulsa World* about the players being fat—did any of the Royals learn of it?"

Ted felt his face flush red. He had been ready for the standard question, Why aren't you playing more often? But he was not expecting a question about the interview.

He swallowed hard and said, "Yes, they learned of it—all of them."

"Did it cause problems?"

"Well, it sure didn't help any."

Coach Greene smiled. "Now you know why I've never allowed my players to give interviews to the press."

Ted nodded. "Yeah. I thought of that at the time—but too late."

Then came the question Ted was expecting: "You're not playing very much, are you?"

Coach Greene's advice did not come as a surprise to Ted: "Hang in there. Hank Quincy may have something in his mind that he's not talking to you about. He may have his good reasons for keeping quiet. One of them may be simply to see how you handle yourself."

"Maybe," Ted said. "At least, that's what I've been trying to tell myself for a month."

At dinner the subject of college resurfaced in the Bell household. Ted was telling his parents about his teammates, and, yes, Lou Mills, when his father spoke up.

"What do you think is going to happen to Lou Mills—or, more to the point, to you?"

Ted paused a moment, then said, "I don't know." He realized that he had been saying that a lot lately.

"You sort of thought, didn't you, that Mills was going to retire, or that the Royals were going to trade him?"

"Yes. Yes, I had that idea. I thought I was joining

them to play—to get a chance. But now I don't know."
There was that phrase again.

"The Royals haven't given you any indication of their plans? I mean, they haven't said anything—nothing at all—about what they're planning for you?"

"No, nothing." Ted remembered Quincy's cutting question—"You're getting paid, aren't you?"—in his ill-fated interview with the manager. "I guess they figure that if they're paying me, I haven't got any grounds for complaint."

"Umm." His father was frowning. "And Lou Mills just keeps playing third base."

"He sure does."

"And you keep riding the bench."

"That's about it."

"With no sign of change."

"None that I know of."

"Where do you think all this is taking you?"

Ted tried to think of something to say other than his new most-often-used expression. But he couldn't. He said, "I don't know."

His father nodded. "Well, as I told you, we've enrolled you at Oklahoma State. Just in case."

"Yes."

"You've got a month to figure it out."

Ted nodded. "Maybe something will happen."

"You've got a lot of thinking to do."

"Yes." Then he added, without thinking, "Thanks," He had spoken the word before he knew what he was saying. But he knew he appreciated his father's not hammering away at him about leaving his bench-riding role with the Royals and going to college.

The Nationals were leading 2–1 when Lou Mills stepped up in the fourth inning for his second at-bat in the All-Star Game. He had lined a double to deep left center in his first trip to the plate, sending home the Americans' only run. And now settling into the batter's box, waggling his huge bat, he looked ready to belt the ball outside everyone's reach. Muscular, confident, he was a menacing figure at the plate.

The Bells' family room was crowded, with all eyes on the television set. A group of Ted's friends and some neighbors had gathered to cook hamburgers on the charcoal grill alongside the patio, then had moved inside the house to watch the game. Ted, Charlie, and two other former Genoa High teammates sat cross-legged on the floor in a semicircle in front of the set. Coach Greene and his wife were on one sofa, and a neighbor couple was on another. Ted's mother was in a chair next to the Greenes. Ted's father was standing, leaning against the door jamb.

Curley Collins, the Cardinals' ace, was on the mound for the Nationals. He was off to a wild start in his three-inning stint, walking the first batter he faced on four straight balls and going to a 3–0 count on the second before getting him on a high fly to right field. His first two pitches to Mills missed the plate, and the catcher, the Cubs' Pete Jenkins, walked out to the mound to try to calm him down.

Mills stepped out of the batter's box and tapped at his shoe with his bat while the pitcher and catcher talked on the mound.

Jenkins returned to his position behind the plate and lowered himself, ready for the pitch. Mills stepped back into the batter's box and glared at the pitcher.

Collins leaned forward and stared at the catcher's signal. The television camera zoomed in on his face, revealing a frown that showed concern. Then Collins straightened, went into his windup, kicked, and pitched. It was a fastball, inside. Mills stood his ground. Then he suddenly leapt back—but too late. The ball hit something—the handle of the bat or Mills—dropped to the ground, and trickled across the third-base line. Mills dropped the bat and bent over. He was clutching his left hand in his right.

Two trainers rushed toward the plate. They said something to Mills. He said something. Then they led him to the dugout.

Ted stared at the television screen, expressionless.

Nobody in the room said a word.

CHAPTER

10

The television announcers babbled something about the injury possibly being serious, or possibly not being serious, and promised to tell the world the news the moment they knew.

A runner took first base for Lou Mills, advancing the previously walked batter to second base, and the next hitter stepped into the batter's box.

"You might find yourself playing third base," Ted's father said from behind him.

Without turning, Ted said softly, "Maybe."

He hoped he sounded calm. Inside, he was anything but calm. The injury looked like a bad one to him. The picture of Lou Mills, bent over in pain, being led away by the trainers, was a chilling one. Indeed, the Royals might be needing a new third baseman on the field.

Nobody else spoke. On the screen, the game resumed. Everyone watched silently as the batter drew a base on balls, loading the bases with one out. Curley Collins headed for the showers, his appearance in the All-Star Game a brief disaster.

A grounder to the shortstop set up an easy double play, spiking the threat by the Americans.

During the lull in the action while the teams changed sides, the announcers reported that nobody knew anything about Lou Mills's condition yet.

At the end of the sixth inning one of the announcers—Harry Broadman—said, "We've got the word on Lou Mills's injury now, and it's bad news."

The Bells' family room fell silent again. Ted stared at the announcer, whose face was wearing an appropriately glum expression. He paused, playing the dramatic moment for all it was worth.

"The doctors tell us that the middle finger and the third finger of the left hand are broken and he'll be sidelined for at least a month."

Ted felt his heartbeat quicken. In less than forty-eight hours from this moment, in Yankee Stadium in New York, he was going to be the third baseman for the Kansas City Royals. His chance had arrived. An unfortunate, perhaps even tragic, accident had provided his opportunity.

As he stared at the announcer's face Ted recalled all the times he had watched Lou Mills and thought him a step too slow. He wondered now if a younger, quicker

Lou Mills might have escaped the wild pitch. A younger man's reflexes might have made a couple of inches of difference—all the difference in the world. Being a flicker of a second too slow had cost Lou Mills a serious injury, and maybe his job.

The other announcer—Van Hunter—began an analysis of the significance of Lou Mills's injury.

"This comes at the worst possible time for the Royals," he intoned in a somber voice. "The Royals are floundering around in sixth place in the American League West. If they're going to make a move for the division championship, this is the time to begin it—now, coming back from the All-Star break."

Van paused, and Harry leapt into the breach. "It's common knowledge," he said, "that Hank Quincy is in a win-or-else situation this year."

"Yes," Van said, recapturing control. "Somewhere someone probably has already drawn up the veteran manager's walking papers, ready to deliver them if he falls short of leading the Royals into the playoffs, and maybe even if he fails to get them into the World Series."

Harry nodded thoughtfully and commented, "And now Quincy has to try to do it without his great third baseman."

Van Hunter picked up the line of thought and asked, "Who've the Royals got to put in for Lou Mills, Harry?"

Ted stared fixedly at the television screen, waiting for

Harry's reply. He imagined that he felt all the eyes in the room on him, watching for his reaction.

"Well, as I see it," Harry said, "Hank Quincy has got two choices."

Two? Ted blinked at the announcer.

"There's Ted Bell, an untried rookie who's been with the team since early June," Harry Broadman said. "The Royals took Bell in the summer draft, and he joined the team after graduation from high school. The Royals are high on him. He's strong and quick, a good fielder and a powerful hitter." He paused. "Matter of fact, Bell hit a home run in his first time at bat with the Royals— poled one of Buster Krump's fastballs out of the park as a pinch hitter. But he's untried, really a question mark. No, Ted Bell, for all his good prospects, would be a big gamble for the Royals at this stage."

Ted frowned. He had never before been referred to as a big gamble on a baseball field. Ted Bell was a sure thing on a baseball field.

"And what's the other choice, Harry?"

Yes, what? Who? Ted held his breath. What was Harry talking about—another choice?

"Jerry Meadows," Harry announced.

Ted blinked again. Who?

"Jerry Meadows is the third baseman with the Royals farm club at Omaha," Harry continued. "He's caught fire this year, fielding well and hitting .389. He had a so-so year at Jacksonville last year but seems to have come into his own this year with a higher classification club. He looks like he's ready. Hank Quincy may decide to go with Meadows, who's in his third year of professional ball and has shown he can produce in the grind of playing every day."

Ted's heartbeat slowed back to normal. For all he knew, it quit beating. He felt all the air go out of his lungs. He stared blankly at the announcer's face on the television screen, unable to believe that his soaring hopes had plummeted so quickly. He felt a little dizzy.

"You ever hear of Jerry Meadows?" Charlie asked from alongside Ted.

Ted shook his head. "No," he said, not taking his eyes off the television screen.

Ted's mind went back to the long days and nights of sitting on the bench watching Lou Mills play third base. He had found it frustrating. Now he tried to imagine sitting there and watching somebody named Jerry Meadows perform through nine innings, day after day, night after night.

Van chimed in, "So you think it'll be Jerry Meadows, up from Omaha, eh, Harry?"

"Can't say for sure," the announcer replied. "While Jerry Meadows is looking good and has the experience over Ted Bell, the folks in the Royals' front office are convinced they've got a real find in Bell—one of those once-in-a-lifetime players, the likes of a Mickey Mantle or a Joe DiMaggio coming on the scene."

Charlie whistled softly and said, "Jeez! Mickey Mantle, Joe DiMaggio—and Ted Bell! All in the same breath!"

Ted couldn't help smiling slightly. He had to admit he liked the sound of it. But he said, "We'll have to wait and see, I guess."

Harry, as if he had heard Ted's comment and thought it a good point, looked into the camera and said, "We'll have to wait and see. Right now we don't have any idea what Hank Quincy's thinking on the matter might be."

"And," Van said, "adding to the unanswered questions, there's always the chance the decision won't be Quincy's, anyway."

"That's right. The people in the front office might tell Quincy to go with Ted Bell, no matter what his preference is. It seems unlikely they'd overrule their field manager, but anything is possible. Either way you can be sure that Quincy will have his say in the matter. He always does."

Ted wondered about the faceless people in the front office who seemed to be fans of his. And he wondered about Hank Quincy, whose only response to Ted's ambitions had been, "You're being paid, aren't you?"

The announcers backed off their between-innings chatter and speculation when the pitcher concluded his warm-up tosses and the first batter stepped to the plate for the start of the seventh inning.

"I'm betting that you'll get it," Charlie said. "Wow! Mickey Mantle, Joe DiMaggio—and Ted Bell!" Then he added, "Who's Jerry Meadows, anyway?"

Ted grinned at Charlie, then turned and looked at his father.

Mr. Bell shrugged.

Ted knew what was in his father's mind. Jerry Meadows, someone he'd never even heard of, just might turn out to be Ted Bell's ticket to a freshman year at Oklahoma State.

At the start of the eighth inning the two announcers assured the television audience that they were doing everything possible to reach Hank Quincy. But nobody was answering Quincy's home telephone in Kansas City, and he wasn't registered in any of the leading hotels in San Francisco, which probably meant he was not somewhere in the crowd watching the game.

But they were going to keep trying to find the Royals manager, they said, and they promised an immediate report if successful.

In the end, the Americans won the game 4–2.

The announcer never located Hank Quincy.

CHAPTER

11

Ted did not sleep well.

Finally, with the first of the sun's rays, he got out of bed. He stepped into a pair of jeans, pulled on a T-shirt, slipped his bare feet into moccasins, and went downstairs. With his parents still asleep, the house seemed empty and quiet. He walked through the family room and stepped outside onto the patio. The morning was cool. But the sky was cloudless, signaling the coming of another scorcher, the usual for Oklahoma in July. Ted sat down at the redwood table.

This was the final open day of the All-Star break. This time tomorrow Ted and his parents would be getting into the car for the short drive to Tulsa and his flight to rejoin the Royals in New York.

And then what?

Chin on his fist, Ted squinted into the bright morning

light. He tried to see into the future. Not all of it. Just a few days. Maybe a week.

But all he saw was the picture of Lou Mills, his face twisted in pain, bending over, his right hand clutching his left. And then, out of nowhere, a couple of trainers appearing to lead him off the field and down through the dugout.

The television announcers' faces then appeared in Ted's mind. They took turns saying, "Jerry Meadows . . . Jerry Meadows . . . Jerry Meadows." It was like a dream.

Ted wondered if anyone had ever found Hank Quincy. And if so, had the manager said anything about who might be playing third base for the Kansas City Royals during the next month or so?

Maybe in Omaha, or somewhere, at this very moment, a third baseman named Jerry Meadows was packing his bags for a flight to New York. Maybe Jerry Meadows had received a telephone call telling him he was going to play in Yankee Stadium tomorrow night. Ted Bell was going to sit on the bench and watch him play.

"You're up mighty early."

Ted turned with a start and saw his mother standing in the door, wearing a yellow cotton robe over her nightgown.

"I couldn't sleep." Ted got to his feet.

"Your father's shaving," she said. "I'll dress and then start breakfast."

She disappeared from the door, and after a moment Ted turned and walked around the house to see if the morning *Tulsa World* had arrived. He was standing in the driveway when a boy on a bicycle, his newspaper bags draped over the handlebars, pedaled past and lightly tossed a rolled-up paper to him.

Ted caught the paper in his left hand.

"Hi, Ted," the boy said, and pedaled on.

"Hi," Ted replied. He was sure he never had seen the boy before. But the boy knew about him. Everyone in Genoa knew about Ted Bell. They all knew that he had gone away to play third base for the Kansas City Royals. But now perhaps everyone in Genoa, and the whole world, was going to find out that Ted Bell was not the next third baseman for the Royals. Ted carried the rolled-up paper inside.

He sat on the sofa and opened the paper to the sports page.

His mother walked through the room. She was wearing maroon slacks and a loose-fitting light blue shirt. "Anything in the paper?"

"Just got it."

"Breakfast is coming up." She walked into the kitchen.

The sports page had a photograph of an injured Lou Mills with the two solicitous trainers peering at him. The story announced the old news that he had suffered two broken fingers and faced at least a month on the sidelines.

Next to the main story was a small headline that asked a simple question: IS IT BELL?

Ted folded the page back and leaned forward, reading the story.

The story identified Ted and gave his baseball background, adding, "With the veteran Mills performing at his usual All-Star clip, the rookie Bell has played infrequently."

Ted mumbled, "You can say that again."

"What's that?" his father asked, suddenly appearing on his way to the kitchen.

Ted looked up. "Nothing," he said, and smiled. "Good morning."

"Any word on anything?"

"No. Not really."

"No word from Quincy?"

"Nope."

"You ought to know something before the day is out, shouldn't you?"

Ted shrugged. "I hope so."

His father walked into the kitchen and poured himself a cup of coffee.

Ted turned back to the story under his headlined name. It mentioned Jerry Meadows of the Omaha farm club as a possibility. But it did not answer the question, "Is it Bell?" Worse, the story added another possibility. Ted frowned as he read. "The Royals may decide that neither

Bell nor Meadows is what they want and go to the trading block to find themselves a third baseman with major league experience to fill in for Mills."

Ted had not thought of that. Neither, apparently, had the two television announcers of the night before, who had dragged out all the speculation they could muster.

Ted laid the paper aside and walked into the kitchen to wait for breakfast.

After eating, he turned on the television set. He twirled the dial, but he found nothing new. The shows offered nothing more than reruns of the wild pitch, Lou Mills's frantic leap backward, and then the awful moment of bending over, clutching his injured hand. "No word yet on who will replace Mills," they all said.

Throughout the morning Ted left the radio on, the volume turned down, waiting for a newscast to tell him about his future. But the announcement never came.

The telephone rang three times that morning. He always almost leapt to answer, hoping it was Hank Quincy. But each time the caller was a sports reporter—one from the *Tulsa Tribune* looking for a fresh angle for the afternoon paper, one from the *Daily Oklahoman* in Oklahoma City, and Buzz Kirby, the sports editor of the *Genoa Mirror*.

At noon he told his mother not to plan on him for lunch. He was going to drive out to Lake Hobson and would grab a hot dog with Charlie on his lunch break.

"Thank goodness," his mother said.

"What?"

"You've done nothing but twitch and fidget around here all morning. It'll do you good to get out for a while. Besides, I'm afraid you're going to injure yourself jumping for the telephone every time it rings."

"If I should get a call—"

"I know. I think I can manage to take a message."

"Yeah. Okay."

At Lake Hobson, Charlie, perched atop his lifeguard chair, greeted Ted with, "Any word?"

"Nope. Nothing."

"Jeez, you'd think the guy would let you know one way or the other."

"You don't know Hank Quincy. You about ready for your lunch break?"

"Yeah, here comes my relief now."

Then the afternoon dragged by, and then the evening, and then the night, and then the next morning. There were three more calls from sportswriters, one from Coach Greene, and, late in the evening, a call from Charlie.

But there was no call from Hank Quincy.

Ted, with his carry-on bag in his right hand, emerged from the ramp, turned to his right, and began walking briskly through the corridors of La Guardia Airport toward the cab stand out front. He was frowning. It was now almost forty-eight hours since everyone in the world—and presumably that included Hank Quincy—had learned that Lou Mills was going to be sidelined for at least a month with an injured hand. But if the manager had decided on a new third baseman, he hadn't told anyone. Or if he had told, the word had not reached Ted.

Ted had watched the early-morning news on television before he and his parents left for the Tulsa airport. There was nothing. He had scanned the morning paper. But there was nothing—not even speculation this time. He had given the telephone one last look as he walked out of the house. It just sat there, silently.

Weaving through the crowds in the concourse, he passed a newsstand and, without thinking, veered toward it and bought a copy of the New York *Daily News*.

With the paper in his left hand and the bag in his right, he stepped back into the flow of people moving through the terminal. Then he stopped. He moved to the side, toward the wall. He put the bag on the floor and looked at the newspaper. The mayor of New York was saying something about water usage in big black letters. Ted turned to the back page and stared at a huge picture of a woman tennis player charging the net. He turned the page, opening up to the sports section.

The black headline jumped out at him from the top of the page: IT'S BELL, QUINCY SAYS.

Ted folded back the page. He felt his heart begin to pound. His face broke into a wide smile.

Ted began to read the story: "Hank Quincy of the Kansas City Royals came to town today and announced that rookie Ted Bell is his choice to replace the injured legend, Lou Mills, at third base."

"Wow!" Ted said under his breath. He looked around. He wanted to shout the news to someone, anyone. But he didn't.

He looked back at the headline: IT'S BELL, QUINCY SAYS.

Ted leaned his head back, looked at the ceiling, and shouted, "O-kay!"

Some of the people moving by glanced at him but kept going.

CHAPTER

Ted arrived early at Yankee Stadium.

Game time was more than three hours away when he got out of the cab, straightened and looked up, and took in his first sight of Yankee Stadium. It was the "house that Ruth built," the home field for Babe Ruth, Lou Gehrig, Joe DiMaggio, Mickey Mantle—the most famous baseball stadium in the world. It was a magnificent sight. And, Ted thought as he stared at the edifice, it was a long, long way from Genoa, Oklahoma. Tonight he was going to play third base, and bat, in Yankee Stadium.

Carrying his garment bag, folded and buckled, he hurried across the sidewalk and along the wall of the stadium to the players' gate.

The gate was closed with a loop of heavy chain connected at the ends with a large padlock. Ted rattled the gate to no avail. He looked through the chain-link gate, to the left and to the right. The place was empty. But surely someone was around. He considered walking around the stadium, perhaps to a ticket window or to a gate where the maintenance crews entered. Then a man in khaki pants and shirt, wearing a Yankees cap, came down a ramp, turned, and started walking away from Ted.

"Hey!" Ted shouted.

The man kept walking.

"Hey!"

The man stopped, turned, and gave Ted an indifferent look. "Gate's not open yet," he said, and started to turn and walk away.

"I'm Bell—Ted Bell—of the Royals."

The man walked slowly toward Ted, giving him an uncertain look. "You're who?"

"Ted Bell, the Royals' third baseman."

"A little early, aren't you?"

"Yes. But let me in, will you?"

The man stared at Ted another moment. Then he pulled a huge ring of keys out of his hip pocket, selected one and unlocked the padlock, pulled the chain through, and opened the gate.

Ted stepped inside. "Thanks," he said.

Without answering, the man looped the chain through the gate, slipped the padlock into place, and slammed it shut.

"Which way's the visitors' dressing room?"

The man gestured to his left, then stood and watched Ted walk toward the door.

The dressing room was empty. Ted dropped his garment bag on a bench and began looking for the number-five stall. When he found it, he stood still a moment and looked at his uniform.

Ernie Rome waddled out of the ramp and gave Ted a surprised look. "Afraid you were going to be late?" he asked.

Ted grinned. "No. I wanted to look around. I've never seen Yankee Stadium."

"Well, this is it."

Ted paused for a moment, half expecting the equipment manager to say something—a word of congratulation or good wishes, perhaps. But Ernie walked across to a table holding stacks of towels and began moving them around, as if Ted didn't exist.

"I'm playing tonight," Ted said finally.

Ernie looked up at him. His face was a blank. "Yep. I saw it in the paper," he said.

"Well?"

"Well, what?"

"Aren't you supposed to say 'congratulations' or 'good luck' or something like that?"

"Good luck," Ernie said flatly.

Ted watched the trainer as he turned back to the towels. The sourpuss never had a good word for anyone. Matter of fact, except for Cal Hanley and occasionally Brian Stevens, nobody on the team had a good word for anyone.

Why?

For a while Ted had thought the animosity, the indifference, the coldness were aimed at him, the rookie hotshot brought up by the front office. But in time he had come to see that except for a few personal friendships, the Royals seemed to care nothing about each other, the team, or the game.

"What's with you?" Ted asked. "You and everyone else."

"What do you mean?"

Ted shrugged and said, "Oh, nothing," and walked away. He wasn't here to probe the trainer for answers. What did Ernie Rome know, anyway? Ted was here to look at Yankee Stadium—and then to play here.

He sighed and said, "I'm going to have a look around."

Ernie, without looking up, continued to move towels around.

As Ted crossed the room and walked the length of the ramp leading to the dugout, he let the image of his teammates and Ernie Rome's words slide out of his mind.

Coming out of the ramp into the dugout, Ted peered across the field—at the green grass of the infield; at the pitcher's mound; at the smooth, brown dirt of the base paths; at the distant outfield wall; at the rows and rows and rows of grandstand seats.

He stepped out of the dugout and stood near the on-deck circle, looking at third base. It looked like any third base Ted ever had seen—a square canvas pad, fifteen inches by fifteen inches. But somehow it was different. So was the grass, the dirt, the pitcher's mound. This was, after all, Yankee Stadium. Ted remembered the famous pictures of Babe Ruth swatting one out of the park. He remembered the smooth swing of DiMaggio, evident even in a still photograph. Ted felt himself in the presence of bigger-than-life ghosts.

He turned and stepped back through the dugout and up the ramp to the dressing room to begin changing into his uniform for the game.

The room was filled with men in various stages of changing from street clothes into baseball uniforms. Ted, dressed, was tying a shoelace.

Of all the men around him, only two of them had said anything to indicate they knew, or cared, that Ted Bell was taking over at third base.

Cal Hanley had entered the dressing room looking for Ted. Spotting him, he had grinned, winked, and made a circle of his thumb and forefinger. He walked straight across the room to Ted. "Great news!" he said.

"Yeah," Ted said, smiling back at the older pitcher. "Nervous?"

Ted shrugged. "No, not really," he said, knowing he was not as certain as he was trying to sound.

"Really?"

"Maybe a little," Ted said with a grin.

"Good. That helps. A little nervousness is a good thing." Ted nodded.

"You'll be great," Cal said.

"Sure."

A few moments later Freddie Hanover, still in his street clothes, had sought out Ted. But Freddie was neither smiling nor gesturing. He was all business. "Watch me," he said, "and I'll help position you for the hitters. You know, like last time."

"Sure," Ted said. Then he added, "Thanks."

Freddie started to walk away and then turned back to Ted, as if he had forgotten something. "Good luck," he said.

"Thanks."

Most of the players were dressed, and some, including Ted, already were ambling out the ramp when Brian Stevens burst through the door. He moved quickly to his stall near Ted's and began ripping off his street clothes. "Plane was late," he said to Ted almost breathlessly.

From behind them the voice of Hank Quincy, making his pregame prowl through the dressing room, squeaked, "Glad to see that you decided to join us this evening, Stevens."

Ted turned to Quincy, but Brian, without turning, looked at the ceiling. "Plane trouble," he said. "Sorry."

"You've had three days to make it to New York. Perhaps you could have arranged an earlier flight."

"Yeah," Brian said, continuing to undress, still with his back to the little manager. He peeled off his shirt and hung it up.

Quincy looked at Ted. "You ready?"

"Yes, sir."

Quincy stared at Ted for a moment and then turned and walked away without another word.

"Whew!" Brian said. "I didn't think I was going to make it. The plane was late leaving Kansas City and then got stacked up over New York."

The dressing room was emptying now. Ted sat down on a bench to wait for Brian.

"I saw the papers," Brian said, pulling his shirt on over his head. "So you're it for the duration, huh?"

"Yep, I guess I'm it."

Brian poked one leg, then the other, into his pants, and leaned close to Ted with a silly leer on his face. "Been busy receiving the congratulations and best wishes of all your teammates, I suppose."

Ted looked at Brian and frowned. "Well, I—"

"I know, I know," Brian said, without looking up. "It happened to me a couple of years ago. Ol' Leroy Snelling developed a sore shoulder and then needed surgery, so I got the job, and all of a sudden everyone looked at me like I had leprosy."

"Why?"

Brian turned to Ted. "Part of it is the fact that the old-timers don't like to see one of their kind shoved aside by a new kid. They all know that their day is coming, that their time is running out, too, but they don't like to be reminded of it."

"And the other part?"

"Huh?"

"You said that was part of it. What's the other part?" Ted thought he knew the answer, but he wanted to hear what Brian thought.

Brian finished tying his second shoe and stood up. "You know," he said. "You've seen 'em."

They walked toward the ramp leading to the dugout.

CHAPTER

13

Ted went 3 for 4 at the plate. His line-drive double to right center field drove home Brian Stevens for the game's first run in the first inning. He scored a run himself in the fifth inning, singling and then trotting home when Eddie Patterson blasted a fastball out of the stadium. Then, in the ninth inning, Ted's single over the shortstop's head kept alive the Royals' rally for the two runs that won the game. The final score was 5–4. In the field, Ted played without error. He made two outs, catching a high pop foul and spearing a line drive to his left, and made three assists, one of them part of a double play.

For Ted the performance was near perfect. And at the finish—a slow grounder that Brian gobbled up and tossed over to Eddie Patterson—Ted was pounding his glove with his fist and letting out a whoop of victory as he turned and ran toward the dugout.

For the Royals as a team, the performance was close enough to perfect—a victory. But none of the others let out a whoop of victory. They nodded as if they had concluded some sort of routine business deal. None of them ran toward the dugout. The outfielders jogged in casually, and the infielders thrust their gloves into their hip pockets and walked.

Ted slowed as he approached the dugout and turned to watch his teammates. He knew what Coach Greene would say to them: "If you're too tired to run at the end of the game, I'll give you a rest next time we play." But Hank Quincy not only didn't say anything, he wasn't even there to watch. He had vanished into the ramp leading to the dressing room about the time the grounder made its first bounce on the way to Brian's glove.

Freddie Hanover caught up with Ted. "Nice game," he said.

Ted turned, almost in surprise. "Thanks," he said. "And thanks for the help." The shortstop's waving signals had placed Ted in the right position for the Yankee hitters.

"Sure," Freddie said, walking past Ted and through the dugout.

Ted followed Freddie into the ramp. Behind him on the concrete floor, he heard the cleats of the other players. In the dressing room, Ted walked to his stall, threw a leg over a stool, and sat down. He watched the other players stream into the dressing room.

There were no shouts, no laughter, no wisecracks, no grins. The Royals were as silent and somber in victory as in defeat. Another day's work was done.

Cal Hanley came in. He gave Ted a smile and a wink. But he looked tired. He had come on in the seventh to finish the game. He looked relieved that it was over.

Brian Stevens entered, as businesslike as the rest of them, and walked across to his locker next to Ted's.

Ted wanted to stand on a bench and shout, "We beat the Yankees!" But he sat in place, wondering why nobody on this team wanted to shout and laugh.

He remembered the first inning, when Brian led off the game with a bouncer through the box for a single. Ted, carrying a weighted bat into the on-deck circle, had called out, "Hey, baby! Attaway!" He was sure Brian's hit was a good omen. The Royals were going to roll over the Yankees in Ted Bell's first game as their regular third baseman. Then he realized his shout was the only one. The other Royals were accepting Brian's single as routine business. Ted swung the weighted bat in silence.

Mike Bedford, batting second, advanced Brian with a slow grounder that dribbled out to the second baseman. Brian, with a good lead off first base, turned on the speed to try to avoid a double play. The Yankees' second baseman, rushing forward for the ball, grabbed it with his right hand and threw out Mike at first base. Brian pulled up at second.

Ted stepped to the plate and powered the first pitch—a chest-high curve—on a line drive deep into right center field. Brian, off with the crack of the bat, was rounding third base as Ted turned at first. Brian scored standing up, and Ted ran to second with a stand-up double.

Ted, edging off second base, glanced at the dugout while Eddie Patterson, the cleanup hitter, lumbered to the batter's box. The Royals should have been on the edge of the dugout shouting. They had one run, a man on second with the cleanup hitter at the plate, and only one out. They were leading the Yankees in the first inning. So they had plenty to cheer about. But nobody was at the edge of the dugout. Nobody was shouting. And Ted remembered what he had been seeing since the day of his arrival.

Eddie swung from the heels twice and missed. Then he caught a piece of a slider and sent a weak grounder to the first baseman. The first baseman stepped forward, scooped up the ball, took two steps to his left, and kicked the bag, making the out. He turned and glanced at Ted, now returning to second base.

As for Eddie, he was already halfway back to the dugout. He had decided the grounder was a sure out, not worth the effort of running.

Ted, one foot on the bag, watched the big first baseman's departing back. He felt a mix of shock and disgust. He had seen Coach Greene pull a player from a game and send him to the showers for not running out a hit. Ted looked at Hank Quincy, but the manager wasn't even looking at Eddie. He was concentrating on Jim Graham, the designated hitter, moving to the plate.

Graham flied out to left field, and the rally ended.

In the fifth inning, when Ted rapped a single between shortstop and third base and then came home on Eddie's towering home run into the right-field seats, he turned and waited to congratulate Eddie. The first baseman, his belly jostling, circled the bases with his face down. When he crossed the plate and turned toward the dugout, he almost ran into Ted. He looked up, straight into the rookie's face.

"Great, great," Ted had said, reaching out his right hand for a slap.

Eddie, a look of surprise on his face, hesitated a moment. Then he reached out and touched Ted's hand, saying nothing as he continued toward the dugout.

Ted turned and followed him to the dugout, wondering at what age the thrill of a home run disappeared. Somewhere between his own and Eddie's, he figured.

In the seventh inning, when a tiring Barry Christopher gave up two runs and let the Yankees take the lead, Hank Quincy walked to the mound with that bandy-legged stride of his. He spoke with Christopher for a moment. Then he waved at the bullpen for Cal Hanley. Barry Christopher went to the showers.

Ted, without thinking, joined the huddle at the mound—Hank Quincy, Bomba Wright from behind the plate, and Cal Hanley—to give a pat on the back and a word of encouragement. Back at Genoa High, he always walked over to an incoming relief pitcher to wish him luck. Usually one or more of the other infielders did the same. Ted was sure that the reliever, knowing he was in trouble before he started, appreciated the votes of support.

But Hank Quincy looked at the rookie as if he were some strange museum exhibit he could not identify. Bomba Wright, seeming startled by Ted's appearance, stopped speaking in mid-sentence. Even Cal, his face showing the tension provided by the top of the Yankees' batting order, seemed discomfited by the sight of Ted.

"Are you lost?" Quincy asked.

Ted felt his face flush red. "No," he said.

Quincy stared at him.

Ted turned to Cal and reached out with his glove to tap him on the arm. "Good luck," he said.

Cal nodded without speaking.

Ted turned and trotted back to his position at third base. He knew that the eyes of his teammates in the infield and in the dugout were on him. He tugged at the visor of his cap and pulled it a fraction of an inch lower.

While Cal put out the fire—a strikeout and a grounder to Freddie—Ted remained silent in his position at third base, his jaw clenched. But when Freddie threw out the final batter to end the inning, bailing the Royals out of trouble, Ted ran across to Cal, shouting, "Attaway!" and walked to the dugout with him.

Ted's looping single over the shortstop's head in the ninth inning, keeping alive the Royals' game-winning rally, wiped out the memories of it all—Hank Quincy's put-down, Eddie Patterson's refusal to run out an infield grounder, everyone's indifference to everything. Ted, dancing off first base, kept up a line of chatter until Eddie flied out to deep right field.

"You're a real cheerleader, kid," the Yankees' first baseman said.

Ted kept his eyes on the pitcher, who had the ball. He knew better than to let the first baseman distract him. It was a sure ticket to a pickoff. But he was grinning and chattering again after he dashed to second base behind Jim Graham's single to center field.

Despite it all, baseball was fun.

"Hey, what did Quincy say to you on the mound?"

Brian, barefoot and stripped to the waist, was leaning in close to Ted in front of their stalls.

Ted felt the blood go to his head—another blush of embarrassment.

"He asked me if I was lost."

"Good ol' Quincy. He's a real sweetheart."

"Yeah."

Brian stepped out of his uniform pants and reached for a towel. "That sort of thing's simply not done on Hank Quincy's teams," he said. "Not professional, you know."

Ted looked up as Brian moved around him, headed for the showers. "Is that right?" he said.

CHAPTER

14

The Royals lost the next three games to the Yankees. Then they flew home to Kansas City to host a series against the Cleveland Indians. They won the first game, 3–0, on Steve Skinner's three-hitter, then dropped the next two and awaited the arrival of the Baltimore Orioles.

The date was July 18. The Royals' record was forty victories and fifty-one losses. They were mired in sixth place in the American League West.

The Royals went about the business of baseball—five losses in the last six games—in their businesslike way. The dressing room sounds were the same after the lone victory as after each of the five losses. Nobody cheered the victory. Nobody complained about the losses. Nobody laughed. Nobody shouted.

Including, by this time, Ted Bell.

Ted was hitting well—his average bobbing around the

.400 mark, with three home runs—and he was fielding well.

But he did not chatter. He did not cheer. He did not shout. He did not rush out of the dugout to congratulate a home-run hitter. And, for sure, he did not go to the mound to wish an incoming relief pitcher well.

He did not decide to quit chattering and cheering. He simply quit. The vision of Quincy's icy stare and the clipped question—"Are you lost?"—reappeared every time he started to cheer. So he quit. The silence of his teammates, apparently indifferent to the successes and failures on the field, left Ted with a feeling that he was shouting in a vacuum. So he quit shouting and cheering.

If Quincy thought baseball had to be a cold business instead of fun, and if his players all agreed with him, so be it.

Ted played third base, he batted, and he kept his mouth shut and his face frozen in a grim—yes, businesslike—expression.

He did not like it, but he did it.

After the last out in the Indians' 5–1 triumph in the final game of the series, he walked silently through the ramp from the dugout to the dressing room.

One of the players behind him asked somebody if he wanted to join him in a steak dinner at the Golden Cow, and the somebody said yes.

Ted did not bother turning to see who they were. He

walked through the ramp, his cleats clacking on the concrete. He weaved his way through the dressing room to his stall and began undressing for his shower.

Freddie Hanover, walking by, said, "Nice game—too bad."

Ted's solo homer in the fifth had provided the Royals' only run.

Ted smiled slightly and nodded his acknowledgment, then watched Freddie walking away, heading for the showers. In a quiet way, Freddie always delivered compliments when they were due. He seemed ready to come alive and cheer, but he never did it. Not in the business-as-usual aura of the Royals.

Ted wrapped a towel around his waist and headed for the showers.

Brian was coming out of the shower. Their eyes met. Brian gave Ted a funny little smile and shrugged silently as they passed. Like Freddie, Brian seemed ready to come to life and shout, but he seldom did. He went along with the businesslike way.

As Ted stepped under the needles of hot water and lathered up, he knew why Freddie and Brian plodded along with the rest of them. They did not want to be shot down by Quincy. Well, neither did Ted, now.

Ted rinsed and stepped out, a towel around his waist, and walked back to his stall.

"Hustle it up there," Cal said from behind him. "Myrna's waiting. We'll drop you off at your hotel. But first we'll find some steaks somewhere."

Ted turned and grinned at Cal. The relief pitcher was the one bright spot on the ball club. Cal did not shout or cheer any more than the others, it was true. But he always offered a smiling face. And unlike any of the others, Cal openly let Ted know that he liked him. Cal was a friend.

"Be right with you," Ted said, stepping up the speed with which he pulled on his street clothes.

"I'll be outside."

"Sure."

Ted finished buttoning his shirt, stuffed his shirttail into his trousers, stepped into his loafers, plucked the sport jacket off the hanger, and walked out.

Sliding into the backseat of Cal's car, he greeted Myrna and leaned back, suddenly experiencing a strange premonition.

Cal Hanley had something on his mind, something other than steaks and a ride to the hotel for Ted.

Ted did not have to wait long for the first signal of confirmation.

"It's late," said Myrna. "Goodness, eleven-thirty. I think I'd rather go on home. Drop me off, and you two major league baseball players can go eat your steaks. I really don't think I could handle a steak at this hour."

"Really?" Cal asked.

"I think so. If you don't mind."

"Whatever you say."

Cal turned the car onto an expressway, drove to a yellow-brick house in the suburbs, and went inside with Myrna.

Ted, shifting from the backseat to the front, saw lights going on, and then Cal's form outlined in the door.

He came back out, got in the car, and started backing out the driveway. "I think she'll be glad when I quit this game," he said. "It gets old—the travel, the night games." He grinned at Ted. "I've been at it a long time."

Ted said nothing, but he reflected that baseball indeed could seem dull after a few years in the indifferent atmosphere that surrounded the Royals.

They drove almost all the way back to the stadium and pulled in at the Happy Bull Steak House.

Bomba Wright and Jim Graham were seated at a table with their wives. Ted and Cal waved to them as the waiter led them to a corner table on the other side.

After they had ordered, Cal said, "I guess you've been reading all the obituaries the sportswriters are cranking out on poor ol' Quincy."

"Do you think they're right—that he's on the way out, maybe even before the season is over?"

Cal hesitated a moment before answering. "A while

back," he said finally, "I thought there was a very real possibility. Remember when I told you about the heat really being on?"

"Yes."

"But now—no, I don't think they're right when they say that Quincy is on the way out."

"You think he'll finish out the season, at least, then?"

Cal smiled. "I think that Quincy will finish this season . . . and next season . . . and one or two more, maybe."

"Really?"

"Really."

Ted, surprised, thought a moment and then said, "But look at us—sixth place and going nowhere."

"Maybe not—that is, maybe not going nowhere. Maybe we're going somewhere."

"Well, we've lost five of our last six games," Ted said. "That's not exactly a turnaround."

"I think Quincy has found what he needs for a turnaround in the last ten days."

"You do? What?"

"You."

Ted stared silently at Cal a moment. Then he frowned. Then he laughed out loud.

Cal smiled at Ted's laughter and said nothing.

"Me?" Ted said finally. "First, I've been in the lineup for seven games. We won two of them. Does that sound like I'm creating the big turnaround? Hardly. And second, I believe that Hank Quincy's idea of real happiness is to send me packing for Omaha, or worse, maybe all the way back to Genoa, Oklahoma."

Cal continued to smile as Ted spoke. Then he said, "Ummm."

"Yes—ummm," Ted said.

"Hank Quincy likes people who play winning baseball. He detests people who play losing baseball. That's all. He's got nothing against you personally. Matter of fact, he's got a mighty big stake in your success, especially right now."

"Well, I'm not doing so bad. Eleven hits in twenty-eight at-bats—that just happens to be a .392 batting average—and no errors in the field."

Cal grinned again. "You hitters always know your averages—if it's above .300."

"You bet, but has Quincy ever said, 'Nice going,' or anything like that? Not once. Not once."

Cal waved a hand slightly. "That's just Quincy. He wouldn't have congratulated Babe Ruth on the sixtieth homer."

Ted shrugged.

"As for the other—"

"What other?"

"Quincy now knows something that he didn't know before, didn't have any way of knowing before—that he has in you the ingredient he needs for the turnaround."

"Did Quincy tell you that?"

"No, he didn't," Cal said, speaking slowly. "But I've been around for a long time, and I know some things about this game. And I've been around Quincy for a long time, and I think I know him."

Ted waited.

Cal hesitated, seeming to choose his words carefully. "You haven't been the same Ted Bell these last few games."

Ted snorted. "What?" He knew what Cal was talking about. But he didn't think there should be any mystery about Ted not being "the same Ted Bell."

"You've been moping around like the rest of them," Cal said.

"Yeah," Ted said simply.

"Look," Cal said, "this team has got the talent—a tight infield, strong hitters, good pitchers, a near genius as a manager. What it needs is a spark to set it afire—and it's got to be you."

Ted shook his head in amazement.

"And," Cal added, "I think Quincy knows this."

Ted leaned forward. "You saw what happened when I walked to the mound to wish you luck. He froze me out. You saw what happened when I was chattering. Everybody looked at me like I was crazy."

"There's an important difference now."

"Oh?"

"That was all before these last ten days, these last seven games."

"So?"

"Ten days ago you were a rookie, virtually untried, a bit of a high school cheerleader type, and little else. It rankled." He paused. "But now you are suddenly on the brink of becoming this team's leader."

"Leader? I don't get it."

"You're performing. You're hitting . . . what, .392? . . . batting in runs, knocking home runs, fielding perfectly, even brilliantly."

Ted waited, watching Cal.

"In sports, as in a lot of things, that's what makes a person a leader—performance. Nobody becomes the team leader by deciding he wants to be the team leader, or by appointment of the manager or the coach. He becomes the leader by performing."

Ted frowned.

"I've seen it happen before," Cal said, leaning back. "Age and experience have little to do with it. If you perform and handle yourself in the right way, you're the team leader. Nobody has to say so. You're just it. That's all."

"I know what you're saying," Ted said. "I understand, but—"

"I've watched it develop these last ten days, almost inning by inning. Freddie sees it. Brian sees it. And, believe me, Quincy sees it."

Ted thought of Freddie, and then of Brian. "Maybe," he said. He remembered his playing days at Genoa High, now seeming so far away in the past. He had been the acknowledged team leader—because he was the best player. "Maybe," he repeated.

"No *maybe* about it," Cal said. "That is, if you'll do it."

"And you think that Quincy really thinks—"

"Yes, I think Quincy really thinks," Cal said with a smile. Then he added, "You can get a lot of respect from Quincy when you hit and field the way you're doing."

The steaks arrived, and Ted dreaded trying to eat his.

Later, at his hotel, Ted walked through the lobby, stepped into the elevator, and punched the wrong floor. He got off before realizing his mistake. The elevator doors had closed. He punched the button for another try at getting off at the right floor.

"Yeah, team leader," he said aloud.

CHAPTER

L ong before game time the next night, Ted had made up his mind.

The decision was easy. The last six games of grim-faced business on a baseball field had not been fun. And since baseball was supposed to be fun, why not enjoy it? If Hank Quincy turned out not to like it, so what? Who cared?

Besides, there always was the chance that Cal had read the signals the right way. Cal had been in the major leagues almost as long as Ted had been alive. He knew the ins and outs of the game. And he knew Hank Quincy, probably as well as anyone. And if Cal was right, it was worth a chance.

Under the lights, the first Oriole batter gave Ted a quick test of the decision, smashing a line drive straight at him, chest-high.

Ted threw up his glove and caught the ball for the out.

Then he looked up, took a moment to massage the pocket of his glove with the ball, grinned at nothing in particular, and shouted, "Hey! Hey! One down!"

He turned and fired the ball over to Freddie. Freddie gave Ted a funny look and tossed the ball over to Brian. Brian flipped the ball to Eddie at first base and gave Ted a glance.

Well, Ted thought, moving into position for the next batter, here goes nothing.

In the top of the second inning, the Orioles brought down the roof on the Royals' big right-hander, Rollie Barnes. Rollie couldn't get the ball past the Orioles' hitters. The first batter slapped a bouncer through the box, past Rollie, and over second base for a single. The second batter lined a double to left center, with the runner stopping at third, thanks to a healthy respect for Mike Bedford's strong right arm. The third batter rifled a long single down the line in right field, scoring both runners.

And Hank Quincy began mincing his way out to the mound.

Bomba Wright, his mitt under his left arm and his mask dangling from his left hand, started walking out to join the conference.

A frowning Rollie Barnes removed his cap, wiped away sweat on his forehead with the back of his right hand, and awaited the arrival of the manager and the catcher.

Ted, at third base, turned and looked at the scoreboard. The Orioles' 2–0 lead showed there. And the Orioles still had a man on first base with none out.

On the mound, Quincy was doing all the talking. Ted could not hear what he was saying. Rollie, towering over the manager, was frowning silently. Bomba was nodding his head as Quincy spoke.

Then Quincy turned and flopped an arm in a halfhearted wave in the direction of the bull pen. Rollie trooped off the mound toward the dugout, shoulders slumped, headed for the showers, his working day at an end. Cal Hanley approached.

Cal nodded at something Quincy said to him. Then he nodded at something Bomba said.

Bomba turned and started returning to his station behind the plate.

Quincy was still saying something to Cal. Then he quit talking and, with a sharp nod of his head, turned and began walking toward the dugout.

Ted started walking toward the mound.

He kept his eyes focused on a spot somewhere in the lower grandstand, beyond Cal and past Eddie Patterson in his position at first base.

Ted could imagine the expression on Brian's face—wide-eyed surprise. Brian knew what Quincy had said to Ted the last time he walked to the mound with a word of encouragement for Cal.

Ted could guess at Freddie's expression—mild surprise.

And he had no doubts about Eddie's expression—disgust at an unprofessional move by a rookie.

Ted did not dare try to imagine the look on Quincy's face. Nor did he dare to look at the manager to find out.

Cal, with the ball in his hand, was scuffing the mound with his shoe and waiting to take his warm-up pitches. He seemed to be waiting for Ted, and he turned easily when Ted put his gloved hand on Cal's shoulder. There was no look of surprise on Cal's face. Just an easy smile and a wink.

Ted saw Bomba standing behind the plate, mask dangling from his right hand, gawking at him.

"Take it cool," Ted said to Cal. "We'll get 'em."

Cal nodded and said, "You betcha," still smiling.

Ted turned and jogged back to his third base position. While Cal took his warm-up throws, Ted stared at nothing. Then he bent and plucked an imaginary foreign object off the ground and flicked it to his right. For all the world he acted like nothing unusual had happened. Or so he hoped.

Cal put out the fire. First, a strikeout. Ted shouted, "Hey! Hey! Attaway!" His voice echoed through the silent infield. Second, a slow grounder to Freddie's right. The runner advanced to second while Freddie threw out the batter at first. Ted shouted, "Okay! Okay!" Third, a high fly to left field, an easy out.

Ted stuffed his glove in his hip pocket and trotted to the dugout. Brian, Freddie, Eddie, Bomba—all of them eyed Ted in the dugout. But none of them said anything. Ted avoided Quincy's gaze as he dropped into a seat on the bench.

The Royals pulled even at 2–2 in the bottom of the fourth inning.

Harold Johnson, leading off, slammed a two-and-two pitch over the right field wall. Ted, sitting next to Brian, said, "C'mon," and left the dugout to greet the hulking right fielder rounding the bases with his head down. Brian followed Ted, and they both clapped hands with the home run hitter. Harold did not seem surprised. He seemed pleased.

A single by Joe Randolph, followed by a double by Freddie Hanover, got the other run.

For the next three innings neither team mustered a threat.

Then, in the top of the seventh, with the top of the Orioles' batting order coming to the plate, Cal weakened.

The first Oriole batter sent a low fly over Ted's head into short left field for a single. Cal walked the next batter.

Ted watched Cal as the batter flung aside his bat and trotted to first base, sending his teammate to second. The pitcher seemed weary, drawn, flat, as if the strength had suddenly run out of him. He caught the throw from Bomba after the fourth ball with a flopping motion of his arm that seemed to take his last ounce of energy. With effort he turned and almost carelessly glanced at the runners on first and second. The steam seemed to have gone out of him. Then he stepped back off the mound, as if needing a moment to restore himself.

Ted took a step toward the mound. Then he stopped. He glanced at Hank Quincy. He expected to see him coming out of the dugout, heading for the mound. But the manager was making no move toward getting up. Quincy met Ted's gaze. He seemed to nod. It was barely perceptible. But, yes, it was a nod.

Ted jogged across to the mound, waving a glove in the direction of Freddie and Brian.

At the plate, the next Oriole batter stepped back out of the box and busied himself with tapping his cleats with his bat.

Ted tried to smile as he approached Cal.

"Did you hear the one about . . . ?" Ted let the words trail off when Cal turned to face him. The old introduction to the telling of a joke used to work wonders relieving tension in games back at Genoa High. Why not here? But Ted knew when he saw Cal's face that the joke wasn't going to work this time.

Cal smiled weakly at the ancient line. He looked really tired.

Freddie came up behind Ted. Then Brian appeared.

"Hang in there," Ted said. "We'll get 'em."

Freddie, seeing Cal's weariness up close, showed concern in his face.

Brian said, "Plenty of time." But then he openly glanced at the dugout, obviously wondering why Quincy wasn't on the mound replacing Cal.

Cal nodded.

But he didn't get 'em. He walked the next batter to load the bases with none out.

This time Quincy came off his perch at the end of the dugout and walked out to the mound. Bomba joined him.

Cal left, and Dave Monchak came on.

Again, Ted could not hear what Quincy was saying. But one word of Dave Monchak's carried across the infield. He was saying, "Yup." Monchak was oblivious to pressure. He always chewed his gum easily, grinned, and said, "Yup."

When Quincy and Bomba left the mound, Ted ran over, tapped Dave on the shoulder, and said, "Lay it in there."

Dave grinned at Ted, nodded, and moved into position for his warm-up throws.

Freddie and Brian remained at their positions. Maybe

they joined in offering encouragement by invitation only. Ted shrugged at the thought as he settled back into his position.

With the batter up, Ted instinctively moved a couple of steps to his left to accommodate the fact that he was facing a left-handed hitter. Then he inched forward a couple of steps, gambling that he could handle anything coming his way and be a second or two quicker with the vital throw to home plate.

Crouching in position, he glanced back at Freddie.

Instead of waving Ted to a different spot, the shortstop nodded to him.

The Oriole batter dug in his heels and swung on the first pitch, a low fastball on the outside edge of the plate. He connected, a fraction of a second behind the pitch, and sent a sinking line drive to the wrong field, along the third base line.

Ted sprang out of his crouch, going backward. He threw his gloved hand across and dived for the ball. The liner was a low rocket, near the ground. Ted, spinning and falling, got his glove between the ball and the ground.

The batter was out.

Ted scrambled to his knees just inside the baseline.

In front of him, just to his left, stood the startled base runner. He could not break for home base without tagging up at third base. And he could not get past Ted to the base.

Ted reached out with the ball and tagged him.

That was two out.

Leaping to his feet, Ted turned. He saw two blurs in the vicinity of second base—a base runner skidding and reversing gears, trying to get back to the base, and Freddie in a breakneck plunge for the base.

Ted fired the ball to the base.

The ball and Freddie arrived together, a step ahead of the frantic base runner.

That was three—a triple play.

For a moment the whole world seemed quiet.

Ted watched the umpire at second base jerk his thumb in the air, signaling the out.

The world was still quiet.

Then, from the half-filled grandstands, the roar of the cheering fans began rolling down onto the field, sweeping over Ted and the rest of them.

Ted turned and stepped across the baseline, heading for the dugout.

The roar from the crowd continued, growing louder.

Ted saw Quincy in the dugout, He was standing, hands on hips. He was watching Ted. Unsmiling, he nodded his approval of the play.

The cheering continued, and finally Ted touched the bill of his cap with his right hand to acknowledge the roars of the crowd.

Then he was swarmed by players, from the dugout and

from the field. They surrounded him, hands pounding on his shoulders and head.

Ted laughed and ducked into the dugout.

Freddie said, with a touch of awe in his voice, "I never saw one like that."

Eddie Patterson, without speaking, shook Ted's hand. Then the big first baseman grinned and said, "You can go ahead and cheer, kid, if you want to. It's okay with me."

Dave Monchak, true to form, grinned easily and said, "Now that's what I call great pitching—one throw and three outs."

In the end, the Royals beat the Orioles, 3–2, in ten innings, when Eddie Patterson, of all people, beat out an infield hit to score Brian from third base.

CHAPTER

F rom there the Royals went on to win their next seven straight.

They trimmed the Orioles in the next three games, completing a sweep of the series. They rolled over the Toronto Blue Jays, sweeping a three-game series and ending the nine-day home stand. Then they flew to Milwaukee and mauled the Brewers in the opening game of a long road trip.

The string of eight victories lifted the Royals two rungs in the American League West standings, from sixth place to fourth.

They were a bare half game out of third place.

The date was July 28.

And they were on the move.

For Ted, the streak was every bit a personal triumph, as it was a team triumph for the Royals.

In the eight games of the streak, Ted slammed three

home runs and raised his batting average to .406, tops in the American League among those who were playing regularly. Cal cautioned Ted that the "book" on him was still being written by the pitchers and catchers around the league. But Cal added with a grin, "Looks like the book is getting harder and harder to write."

At third base, Ted committed his first fielding error. Officially it was an error. Unofficially it was a topic of hot debate on the sports pages. Ted had dived for a screaming grounder to his left, got it in his glove, throwing off-balance as he fell. His throw was wide, and the official scorer called it Ted's error. The sportswriters screamed in print that a lesser player never would have reached the ball in the first place, that the grounder had "base hit" written all over it, and that the official scorer missed the call. As for Ted, he declined comment. He had learned to watch his words in interviews.

Through the eight games Ted cheered and chattered, clapped players on the back, and slapped their hands when they homered.

Increasingly Freddie and Brian joined in the chatter. And even Bomba Wright, from his post behind the plate, began letting out a whoop of triumph with every strikeout.

Eddie Patterson left the cheering to the others. He was as impassive as ever, but gone was the expression of distaste that met Ted's earlier cheers.

Quincy, watching the Royals roll along, never cracked

a smile, never offered an unnecessary word. Nor did he ever give Ted again as much as a barely perceptible nod.

For Ted, the hitting and fielding and winning and cheering and chattering added up to fun.

But the world was not perfect.

Cal told Ted on the last night of the home stand that he had decided to retire at the end of the season.

"Is that definite?" Ted asked.

The two of them were seated at the Happy Bull Steak House.

"Definite," Cal said. "I've told Quincy. Even told him that I'd quit now if he needed the slot to bring up some strong youngster." He paused. "With the Royals on the move, a strong rookie in the pitching rotation, instead of an old man, would help."

Ted flinched at Cal's reference to himself as an old man. "What did Quincy say?" he asked.

Cal smiled. "Nothing. I don't know what he wants to do."

"When did you decide this?"

"Funny, I happen to know the exact moment."

"Oh?"

"It was when I got knocked out of the box in the first game of the Orioles series. Remember? I had relieved Rollie in the second inning, and I folded in the seventh."

"I remember."

"Heading for the showers, about the time I stepped down into the dugout, I told myself, 'This is it—it's all over.' " He paused. "I decided to sleep on it awhile, didn't discuss it with anyone but Myrna, and I didn't tell Quincy until today."

"Getting knocked out of the box once in a while," Ted said slowly, "isn't the end of the world. It happens to everyone now and then."

Cal chuckled slightly. "Oh, man, I was so tired. I can still go a few innings in relief here and there. But by the seventh inning that night, I could hardly lift my arm."

Ted said nothing. He had seen the pitcher's weariness himself. He could understand Cal's feelings, even his decision. But he found it difficult to imagine life with the Royals without Cal's advice and friendship, without his smile and wink.

"A man can stay around too long," Cal said. "I always considered myself an asset, somebody able to make a contribution, even these last few years. But now I wonder. And nobody wants to be a liability."

"I don't think anyone thinks you're a liability."

"Well, thanks," Cal said. "Say, there was something sort of historic in the game, you know."

"What's that?"

"Maybe you didn't see what I saw."

"What?"

"Quincy risked throwing away the ball game—losing

it—in order to leave me in there for one more batter."

Yes, Ted thought, Quincy did. He remembered that Quincy had remained in the dugout. Cal was worn out, finished. Anyone could see it. Above all, Quincy could see it. Ted had expected to see the manager's mincing stride, heading for the mound to remove the ineffective Cal Hanley. But Quincy had not moved. Except, that is, to give Ted a barely discernible nod. He had left Cal in, and Ted had gone to the mound to prop him up.

"You know what I'm talking about, don't you?"

"I remember he left you in for one batter more than I thought he would."

Cal watched Ted. "He left me in so you would walk to the mound."

"You think so?"

"I know so." Cal leaned forward. "Quincy was willing to let the game get out of reach to make sure you made that walk to the mound, maybe hailing in Freddie and Brian with you. He was willing to invest one game—a loss, if necessary—to get you to make that walk."

"Well, maybe." Ted remembered again the slight nod from Quincy. "Maybe so."

"It was a real turning point. Look what's happened since. Eight straight victories. Up from sixth place to hammering on the door at third. If this team goes to the World Series, and I think we will, the beginning was that walk to the mound."

"Ah," Ted said with a grin, "Quincy probably knew that the next batter was going to hit into a triple play, and none of it mattered, anyway."

Cal laughed. "Either way, Hank Quincy is a genius."

The name of Lou Mills was buried somewhere back in Ted's subconscious memory, under all the hits and catches and throws, and all the triumphs of the past two weeks.

Lou Mills was the name of a man who used to play third base for the Royals.

Ted Bell was the Royals' third baseman.

It was Ted Bell who appeared in color photographs in *Sports Illustrated*. It was Ted Bell whose face appeared on the front page of *The Sporting News*. Ted Bell was leading the league in hitting. He was fielding brilliantly. He was leading the Royals up from the depths of the American League West standings. It was Ted Bell everyone wanted to interview—for the papers, the magazines, radio.

Who was Lou Mills, anyway?

Not even the question, much less a troublesome effort at an answer, had occurred to Ted since the first game of the series with the Orioles, when he pulled off a triple play and Eddie Patterson ran out an infield hit for the victory.

In the course of eight straight victories, the name of Lou Mills had faded into the background.

Then Brian Stevens brought the name back to center stage in their Milwaukee hotel room after the victory over the Brewers in the first game of the series.

"What do you think Quincy is going to do when Lou Mills returns?"

Ted, seated in a chair with the Milwaukee paper spread out on the bed in front of him, looked up in surprise. The name seemed to come out of the distant past. "What?" he asked.

"Do you think Quincy is going to let Mills ride the bench, trade him—or put him back at third base?"

Ted frowned. "I don't know," he said finally. It did not seem possible to Ted that Hank Quincy would bench him. Not now, not after what had happened during the past two weeks—Ted's outstanding playing and the team's winning streak. Ted Bell was leading the league in hitting. How do you bench the league-leading hitter? He was fielding perfectly, with the exception of one disputed call by the official scorer. And he was providing the only spark of life on the team—a spark of life that had helped the Royals to eight straight victories, up from sixth place to within sight of third. No, Quincy could not bench him.

Brian said nothing, watching Ted, waiting for more than the noncommittal, "I don't know."

"Look," Ted said finally, "when the Royals drafted me and agreed to bring me up to the major leagues immediately, I figured that it meant I was going to be the Royals' third baseman." He paused. "At least get a chance, you know."

Brian grinned slightly. "Yeah, that sort of showed right off the bat," he said.

Ted let Brian's remark go by. "Well, Quincy didn't put me in at third base—until he had to. I was surprised. And so now I don't try to outguess him. All of which means I don't have the slightest idea what he's going to do."

"He hasn't said anything to you? You haven't heard anything?"

"No," Ted said. Then a light went on in Ted's brain. He remembered Brian's earlier worrying. "Oh, you mean about second base."

"Yeah. Exactly."

"Have you heard anything?"

"No, I haven't. But the way I figure it, when Lou Mills comes back, Quincy can't bench him. After all, Lou is a baseball legend. He may be getting on in years a bit, slowing down. But remember, he made the All-Star team. So Quincy can't bench Lou Mills. But he can't bench you, either. You're leading the league in hitting. You're a great fielder." Brian stopped and shrugged his shoulders. "Besides, if he tried, the boo birds and the sportswriters, not to mention the wolves in the front office, would tear him apart."

"Well, I don't know," Ted said.

"It seems to me that Mills at third base and you at second is the only answer."

Ted grinned at Brian's frowning face. "You're a worrywart, that's what you are," he said.

Brian's frown stayed in place. "Let me know if you hear anything, will you?"

"Sure."

Later, just before they turned out the light, Ted said with a grin, "Tell you what, let's start the rumor that Quincy is thinking about playing me at first base. If nothing else, it'll scare Eddie."

Brian barely managed a grin.

And Ted's grin faded quickly when he turned out the light and slipped into bed.

Indeed, what was Quincy going to do?

CHAPTER

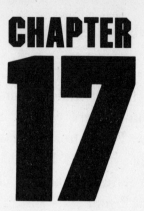

17

atting slumps come on gradually, and they aren't recognized for what they are until they've taken a firm hold. Ted's was no exception.

A strikeout here, a weak infield grounder there, a pop-up now and again—these things happened to all hitters.

Nobody batted 1.000.

Then, at some point, the accumulation of hitless trips to the plate became too much to ignore. The 0-for-4 nights occurred more frequently. The batting average was in a slide. The hitter knew he was in a slump.

Ted was ill equipped to recognize the elements of a hitting slump. He never had experienced one. At Genoa High he hit successfully at least once in every game he'd ever played. With the Royals he had had a couple of hitless games but always bounced back with a strong performance. He was leading the league in hitting.

If a starting point of Ted's slump had to be identified—a point at which the slump was recognizable for what it was—it probably was the third game of the series with the Brewers at Milwaukee.

The Royals won the game, 5–1, and took over third place in the standings by half a game. The winning streak now stood at ten games.

Ted chattered and cheered all the way.

But he went 0 for 4 at the plate, on a routine fly to left field, two infield grounders, and a called third strike.

Elated by the victory and the move up in the standings, Ted thought nothing of his own hitless night. It didn't matter. He would bounce back tommorrow night, and the next night, and the next. He always bounced back.

But Cal was frowning when he approached Ted's stall after the game.

The pitcher was dressed and ready to leave for the hotel. Ted was stuffing in his shirttail and buckling his belt while reliving the victory with Brian.

"Anything bothering you?" Cal asked.

Ted turned with a start. "Me?" he asked in surprise. He was smiling. "What do you mean?"

Cal wore a concerned expression. He seemed to start to say something, then changed his mind. "Nothing," he said finally. "Nothing important."

Ted studied Cal's face a moment, and his smile faded. What did Cal have on his mind?

Then when Cal walked on, Ted shrugged and turned back to Brian.

The next day the Royals flew to Toronto to open a three-game series with the Blue Jays, and fate intervened to keep the secret of Ted's developing slump from being revealed to him. Fate always has had a way of appearing mighty important in baseball on occasion.

Against the Blue Jays in the series opener, Ted walked twice and laid down a sacrifice bunt—none of which was charged as an official at-bat—and singled to left in four trips to the plate.

As far as the statistics keeper was concerned, Ted came out of the game with one hit for one trip to the plate, sending his average up to .397.

A strong performance in the next game would send his average back over the .400 mark—where he intended to finish the season, a rookie batting champion making history, lining up with the likes of Ted Williams.

Ted's thoughts were not the kind that hint of a slump.

The Royals lost the game, 4–0, ending their winning streak. But they clung to third place in the standings, thanks to the Yankees' victory over Minnesota.

Even in defeat, Ted found a reason to cheer silently.

For the first time the Royals were different in defeat. While winning, they had increasingly chattered and joked among themselves in the dressing room. But now, with a loss, a heavy gloom hung over the dressing room.

Ted took heart in the evidence that the business-as-usual attitude seemed to have evaporated somewhere along the way during the winning streak, amid his cheering.

He could hardly wait for the next night—and a return to the winning ways—to see the Royals transform themselves back into a cheering, laughing team.

The next night Ted went 0 for 5, and the following night, 1 for 4. His one hit was a feeble stroke that got past the mound and rolled over second base into center field for a single.

The Royals won both games, one by a 2–1 score when Cal came on in the eighth inning to save the victory for Steve Skinner, and the other by a 4–2 score on Eddie Patterson's home run with two on base.

The victories lifted the Royals into second place.

But Ted was beginning to find it hard to cheer. He had collected a grand total of two hits in fourteen at bats in the last four games. His batting average had plummeted from .406 to .358.

Had the "book" on him been written? Was that it? Had the pitchers around the league learned enough about Ted Bell to get him out twelve out of fourteen times in the last four games? Did this hitless streak mean that the "book" on Ted Bell was completed—and fatally effective?

Ted wanted to ask Cal, but he held back. Increasingly he was afraid of the answer he might get from the veteran pitcher. He started trying to avoid conversation with him—

or meeting his eyes—for fear Cal would provide the dreaded explanation.

And Cal, for whatever reasons, was making no offers.

Suddenly Boyd Hatton always seemed to be there at the batting cage when Ted was taking his pregame warm-up swings.

Silent and unblinking, the great slugger, now the batting coach, stood and watched.

But that was all. He just stood and watched. He said nothing. He did not say, "Try this" or "Don't do that" or "Here's what's wrong." He said nothing. He just watched.

Time and again Ted felt a tremendous urge to step back out of the batter's box, turn to Boyd Hatton, and shout at the top of his lungs, "What's wrong?"

But Ted didn't do it. He kept swinging. Asking what was wrong was the equal of admitting that something was wrong. And maybe nothing was wrong. Nothing serious, anyway. A small, minor problem. Everything was sure to work out. In silence, he kept swinging.

Cal Hanley and Boyd Hatton weren't the only ones keeping their silence. Nobody was saying anything to Ted about his failure to hit. It was as if he had an embarrassing affliction that caused everyone to look away, to ignore him, to refuse to admit its existence.

When Ted and Brian were together in their road-trip hotel room, Brian never mentioned hitting—neither his nor Ted's. And neither did Ted.

Hank Quincy said nothing to Ted, but whenever Ted glanced at the manager, he noticed that Quincy seemed to be watching him closely.

Strange thoughts began to circulate through Ted's mind.

Maybe Hank Quincy liked seeing the upstart high school star take a beating from the pitchers. What harm was done? The Royals were winning without Ted's hitting.

And, Ted thought with a shiver, Hank Quincy knew also that Lou Mills was drawing closer to full recovery with every day that passed. The legend would soon return and reclaim third base, and the high school hotshot would catch a bus to Omaha or Charleston or Jacksonville—a richly deserved trip that everyone would agree was necessary to provide seasoning.

There were thoughts of Brian, too.

The second baseman wouldn't need to worry about Ted's strong bat replacing him in the lineup upon the return of Lou Mills, if Ted's bat were not strong.

The slump was sure to be good news to Brian.

No wonder Brian didn't mention Ted's hitless streak.

There were even thoughts of Cal. The veteran pitcher was hanging up his spikes at the end of the season. Maybe he was, in truth, envious of the hard-hitting newcomer who fielded brilliantly, just starting out in what was sure to be a dazzling career. Maybe Cal was enjoying seeing the hotshot young third baseman who was beating out Lou Mills—an old friend—get his comeuppance.

Eddie Patterson surely liked watching Ted struggle. Ted figured there was no doubt about that one.

Ted's chatter and cheering slowed to a standstill in the course of the last two games against the Blue Jays. It was impossible to be the happy-go-lucky kid when he couldn't hit the ball out of the infield. Who was he to be cheering? Beyond that, when he looked at his teammates and knew what was on their minds, even the thought of cheering and chattering vanished.

Then, as frequently happens during a hitting slump, the batting troubles affected Ted's fielding. He erred twice in the final game against the Blue Jays—first a wide throw to first base, and then a booted grounder.

It was the first time in Ted Bell's life that he had committed two fielding errors in one game.

The next day was August 2, an open date for travel to Detroit for a vital three-game series. With the Minnesota Twins in third place nipping at their heels, and the first-place California Angels only a tantalizing two-and-a-half games ahead of them, the Royals needed a sweep.

A somber Ted Bell sat alone on the plane staring out the window at the carpet of clouds below.

CHAPTER

The players streamed through the lobby of the hotel at noon, following the short flight from Toronto.

Even Ted, in his gloom, noticed the difference in the attention paid to the Royals—now a pennant contender—by the people in the lobby.

"That one's Ted Bell," somebody said as Ted walked by.

Yes, Ted thought. Yes, Ted Bell of the Royals. But not really. Not with two hits in fourteen at-bats. Not with two fielding errors in the last game. Not with everyone on the team enjoying his failures.

Ted picked up his key to the room he would be sharing with Brian and turned toward the bank of elevators. He decided to pass the afternoon of the open day at a movie. Maybe he would take in another one in the evening. Open days in strange cities were a real drag.

He looked up to find himself facing Cal.

"We're going to the ballpark," Cal said.

"What?"

"Get yourself settled in your room and then come on down. We'll meet here in the lobby in twenty minutes."

"It's an open—"

Cal squinted at Ted. "Son, in case you haven't noticed, you're in a slump."

Ted nodded. "I've noticed."

"Good. That's the first step out of a slump, knowing and admitting you're in one. I thought you were never going to figure it out."

"I—"

"Remember the other night when I asked you if anything was bothering you after you went oh-for-four?"

"Uh-huh."

"Well, you were sliding into it, but didn't know it."

"I've never had a slump," Ted said.

"Umm," Cal said. "The best hitters in history have had slumps. You're in some select company. There are two ways out. You can wait it out, or you can work it out." He paused. "This thing has gone on long enough. We can't afford for you to wait it out, so you've got to work it out."

"Okay. Sure."

"We'll meet here in the lobby in twenty minutes," Cal repeated.

"We?"

"You, me, Boyd, and Bomba. I'll throw and Bomba will catch. And Eddie's coming along to watch. Maybe some of the others, too."

"Eddie?"

"He's one of the best pure hitters in the game," Cal said. "A sort of scholar of the science of hitting, if you can believe it."

Ted grinned. His lower lip trembled slightly. He thought for one horrible moment that tears were coming to his eyes. Then he widened the grin and managed to say, "I'll be here waiting for you."

He got on the elevator, hoping that his thoughts of the last two days about his teammates had not been visible on his face.

For almost an hour Ted stood in the batter's box and swung at Cal's offerings.

Bomba worked behind the plate. He occasionally said, "Good" or "Nice one," but nothing else.

Eddie, in sport shirt and jacket, arms folded across his chest above his protruding stomach, stood near the on-deck circle watching. His expression never changed and he said nothing.

Brian and Freddie, also in street clothes, sat cross-legged on the grass near Eddie and watched. Boyd took up his station at the batting cage.

Ted saw Hank Quincy appear in the dugout beyond

Eddie. The manager said nothing—no advice, no encouragement, not even a word of greeting to indicate his presence. He simply stood and watched as Ted swung—again and again and again.

The occasional solid hits felt good to Ted—line drives and one smash that carried over the left field wall.

But he had a gnawing feeling with most of the swings that something—something he could not pinpoint—was not right.

He kept swinging.

After almost an hour Dave Monchak stepped out of the dugout in uniform, carrying his glove. He walked out to the mound, and Cal tossed the ball to him.

Ted stepped out of the batter's box to allow Dave several warm-up throws.

Then he saw Cal walking off the mound, gesturing to him to join the three players in street clothes.

Ted dropped the bat and jogged around the batting cage to meet with Cal, Eddie, Brian, and Freddie. Boyd walked over and joined them.

Hank Quincy had disappeared from the dugout.

"Patience," Eddie said flatly.

Ted blinked. "Huh?"

Eddie took a deep breath and began talking, sounding like a teacher lecturing students. "The toughest thing of all about hitting—successful hitting—is being able to wait until the ball gets into the hitting area without making a false move with some part of your body."

Ted blinked again. He'd never heard such a lengthy sentence out of the taciturn Eddie Patterson. Cal had called Eddie a scholar of the science of hitting. He did indeed sound like a scholar.

"As soon as you make a single false move, you've lost your bat speed."

Ted nodded. "Is that what I've started doing—doing wrong, I mean?"

"Uh-huh. You're starting too soon—just a fraction of a second, but it's enough to mess you up. Be patient. Then go into your move, your swing."

"You make it sound mighty simple."

Eddie glanced at Ted without changing expression. "It's not," he said.

Boyd leaned in. "What Eddie's saying is that the cure to your slump may lie more in a study of your preswing moves than in the swing itself."

Ted nodded. Maybe there had been a change in his moves—infinitesimal but deadly. And, of course, as the slump developed, there may have been more changes in a frantic attempt to correct whatever was wrong. The only thing, though, was that instead of helping, the changes made matters worse.

"And," Boyd said, "I don't want to clutter up your

mind with a lot of advice that just makes things worse, but a lot of your swings aren't level. It's like you're reaching, trying for lift, you know?"

"Uh-huh."

"It's all connected," Eddie said. "In hitting, everything is connected to everything else. And it all starts with the moves you make before the ball has even arrived."

Ted looked at Eddie with new respect. There was, he decided, more than brute strength involved in Eddie Patterson's ability to power a baseball out of the park.

"No slump ever got solved by talking," Eddie said. "Why don't you hit some more?"

The professor's lecture was at an end.

Ted glanced at Cal.

Cal winked at him.

Ted tried to grin at Cal. It didn't quite work.

Ted nodded, turned, and jogged back to the batter's box.

He did not know how many swings were required to cure a slump.

But he was ready to find out.

The Tigers whipped the Royals, 6–1, in the first game of the series. The loss dropped the Royals back into third place.

But the Royals defeated the Tigers in the second and third games and left for Milwaukee solidly implanted back in second place, only one and a half games out of first place.

For Ted, each of the three games of the Detroit series started two hours early, in the late-afternoon hours in an almost empty stadium.

With Cal Hanley or Dave Monchak or Steve Skinner throwing, Ted stood in the batter's box and swung away for an hour.

Bomba squatted behind the plate. Boyd stood behind the batting cage.

Each day Eddie, before changing into his uniform, stood with arms folded across his chest, staring blankly at Ted's swing. He occasionally stepped forward to offer a suggestion. But mostly he just watched.

Each day, too, Brian and Freddie showed up.

Hank Quincy always appeared, watched from the dugout for a few minutes, then disappeared into the dressing room without comment.

Maybe, Ted figured, everyone's silence was part of the process of pulling a hitter out of a slump. For sure, a lot of conflicting advice was not going to help. Neither Eddie nor Brian nor Freddie, could tell Ted how to hit. They could make suggestions. They could point out errors. But it was Ted himself who had to end his slump.

On Tuesday, Ted kept trying to tell himself that more of the hits felt good now than they had on the day before. But he didn't convince himself. There was still something—something indefinable—wrong. He was a fraction of a second off, a fraction of an inch off.

In the series opener, Ted got a hit his first time at bat— a line-drive single to left center field. As he danced off first base he tried to tell himself that the slump was ended, the drought broken. But he went hitless his next four trips to the plate.

The next day, facing the fireball pitching of Dave Monchak in practice, Ted was sure—really sure, this time— that more of his hits felt right. But in the game that night he went 0 for 4.

"It's coming back," Cal said in the dressing room after the game. "Don't worry. It won't be long now."

Ted shrugged. The road out of the slump was beginning to seem very long indeed. "I hope so," he said.

Cal grinned. "You're hitting the ball well. That fly to left in the third would have gone for a home run in some parks. The liner to the shortstop would have gone for extra bases if it had been five feet to either side. You're hitting them. It's just that they're catching them."

Ted reflected, possibly for the first time in his life, that he could use a little luck. But all he said to Cal was, "Yeah."

The next afternoon he slapped the best of Steve Skinner's offerings all over the lot. The hits felt good, no question about it. He caught himself grinning between hits—grinning at Steve, grinning at the blank face of

Eddie Patterson, even grinning at the scowling face of Hank Quincy when the manager appeared in the dugout.

That night Ted singled once, doubled once, walked once, and struck out in four trips.

In the field he chattered and cheered.

After the game Cal said with a grin, "Welcome back."

Ted said, "It's good to be back." He felt good.

Then he walked across the dressing room to Eddie Patterson and said, "Thanks."

"Huh?" Eddie asked.

CHAPTER
19

Then Lou Mills returned.

He was there in the locker room, already in full uniform, when Ted walked in.

The Royals were back home in Kansas City, preparing to open a three-game series with the Milwaukee Brewers following an open date on the schedule.

On the open day, Ted had telephoned his parents. Yes, he said, he had been in a hitting slump. But no, he said, it was behind him now. He had licked it. Yes, he was sure. Yes, everything was fine. And the real reason for the telephone call was, well, he had made a decision. His parents could withdraw the enrollment application at Oklahoma State. He was sticking with the Royals for the duration. He was the Royals' third baseman. The horrible specter of a bus trip to somewhere in the minors was gone from his mind. He would go to college, he told his parents, but in the off-season. Well, all right, they said, if Ted was sure. Yes, Ted was sure.

And Ted *was* sure. He had pulled out of the slump. He was back in the groove—hitting with power, fielding flawlessly, again his old, chattering, cheerleading self, confident and happy.

Beyond the return of his hitting and fielding abilities, Ted was sure for another reason. The picture of Eddie Patterson showing up every day, arms folded over his chest, trying to pull Ted out of his hitting slump, would not leave his mind. There were other pictures, too—Brian and Freddie sitting on the grass, watching; Hank Quincy appearing in the dugout for a few moments; Cal and Steve and Dave spending their pitching arms to lift him out of his slump; Bomba working behind the plate.

Ted was sure about staying with the Royals for more reasons than he could count.

Lou Mills had seldom entered his mind. When Brian, falling occasionally into a worrying mood, mentioned the third baseman, Ted would shrug off the suggestion with a grin. Other times Ted thought of Lou Mills in the same terms he thought of him that first day—trade or retire?

But now, across the dressing room, there he was—Lou Mills in uniform.

A half dozen other players were scattered around the dressing room. Bomba, in his underwear, was seated on a stool, reading a letter. Mike Bedford was seated at the table with the box of baseballs, scribbling his signature on a ball and plunking it back into the box. Brian was standing at his stall, undressing. Eddie, not yet in uniform, was talking to Lou Mills.

Without thinking, Ted looked at Lou Mills's left hand.

No cast, no bandage—nothing. The fingers were mended.

Mills looked relaxed and fit. He was smiling easily as he chatted with Eddie. He was deeply tanned.

Mills spotted Ted and nodded.

Ted nodded back, took a deep breath, managed a smile, and walked across to extend his right hand. "Welcome home," he said. "Is everything repaired?"

Ted felt the eyes from around the locker room on him.

Mills took Ted's hand and they shook.

"Yes," Mills said with a curious smile, "everything is"—he paused briefly—"repaired." Then he said, "You've been doing a good job."

The compliment surprised Ted. Before the injury, the third baseman hardly acknowledged the existence of Ted Bell, much less issued an occasional compliment. For sure, Mills had said nothing about Ted's play the night he was sidelined in the hotel with a head cold.

Ted shrugged and smiled again. "A little trouble hitting these past ten days," he said.

Mills nodded. "Happens to everyone," he said. "But

Eddie says you've got it whipped now—worked your way out of it."

Ted glanced at Eddie, whose face revealed nothing, and then back at Mills, who seemed genuinely interested. Mills's attitude puzzled Ted. He did not seem concerned that his replacement was playing well. He did not seem worried about his job. "Well, I hope so," Ted said. Then he added, "You look like you got some sunshine."

Mills was turning back to Eddie, as if having decided greetings from Ted had come to an end. He looked back and said, "Been float-fishing the Buffalo. Down in north Arkansas, you know."

"Yeah," Ted said. He was increasingly worried by Mills's total lack of concern about the third base job. Mills clearly felt sufficiently confident to hand out compliments, and Ted figured that might not be good news. "Well, again, welcome home," he said.

"Thanks," Mills said.

Ted walked to his stall without asking the question that was burning in his mind: Who's playing third base for the Royals tonight?

Possibly the same question was in Lou Mills's mind.

But maybe not. Mills seemed so confident, so at ease. He did not act like a man with a question in his mind. Maybe he knew he was getting his job back. Maybe he felt he could afford to hand out compliments to his sub- stitute, who was heading back to the bench—a temporary stop until he caught a bus for the minor leagues. Maybe Mills was sure he was going back to third base.

The one man who certainly knew the answer to the question was Hank Quincy, and he was—where? In his office? Already out on the field? Or not here yet? Ted had not seen him.

Had Quincy already drawn up the lineup for handing to the umpire? Would he say anything to Ted? Or would he simply pin up the lineup, same as any other night?

Probably just pin up the lineup like any other night, Ted decided.

At his stall, Ted asked his question aloud. "I wonder who's going to play third base tonight?"

Brian, pulling a sweatshirt over his head, turned to Ted and grinned slightly. "So you noticed who's back?"

Ted did not return the grin. "Have you heard anything?"

"No, not really."

"What do you mean, not really?"

"Just a lot of guessing."

"Nothing from Quincy?"

"Are you kidding? Ol' Closed Mouth? No, nothing."

Ted glanced across at Mills, still chatting with Eddie Patterson and appearing so confident, so relaxed. "Well, then," he said, "what is the guessing?" He figured that anything, even bad news based on nothing, was better than total uncertainty.

"The guessing is, you."

"Really?"

"You're doing the job. Why not?"

Although the players' guesses meant nothing in the face of Quincy's decision, Ted felt a sense of relief. Although the players were not the manager who would decide—and Quincy would not even ask their opinion— they were baseball men. They knew the game. If they thought the rookie was going to be the choice over the legend, well, maybe there was hope, despite Lou Mills's look of confidence.

Ted took off his sport jacket, hung it up, and began unbuttoning his shirt. "I hope they're right," he said.

"So do I," said Brian without looking at Ted.

Ted glanced at Brian. The second baseman was still worried about the vision of Mills at third base—and Bell at second.

Ted said nothing.

"I do tend to worry about second base," Brian said.

"It'll never happen."

And it didn't.

Quincy, without a word to anyone as far as Ted knew, posted the same lineup he'd been hanging up for the past month—Ted Bell at third base, Brian Stevens at second base, Lou Mills unlisted.

In his pregame prowl through the dressing room, Quincy

did not give Ted so much as a nod or a glance. As far as the manager was concerned, the occasion apparently did not warrant advice, comment, or explanation. It was Quincy's job to make the decision, and he had done it. No big deal. It was Ted's job—or Lou Mills's—to play third base. So Ted was going to do it. No big deal. At least that was what Ted told himself.

From the moment he walked over and glanced at the lineup, Ted tried to keep his jubilation inside, hidden. He made his approach to the lineup with an almost exaggerated casualness, as if motivated by nothing more than idle curiosity. When he saw his name—batting third in the order, as usual—he said nothing and kept his facial expression blank. He wanted to cheer, but he didn't. He wanted to smile but he didn't. He wanted to look around for Lou Mills, but he didn't. And he did not linger. He let his gaze cross the lineup and he kept going, although inside, his heart took a leap. He wanted to shout but he didn't.

It was just as well, because his jubilation was short-lived.

He was barely finished with the stretching exercises and into the infield warm-up drills when a chilling thought crossed his mind: Maybe Lou Mills was, after all, Quincy's choice, and Quincy was just giving the veteran a night to settle in before taking up his position.

That, Ted figured with a frown on his face, would

explain Mills's easygoing, untroubled attitude. Lou Mills knew his old job still belonged to him, beginning tomorrow night. Small wonder he seemed unconcerned.

"Something wrong?" Freddie Hanover asked.

Ted wiped the frown from his face. "No," he said.

Ted tried to shake off the fear as he went through the motions of the infield warm-ups. He told himself that it made no sense to delay Lou Mills's return to the lineup for one more game. Why would Quincy do it? No reason. No reason at all. Lou Mills was back, present and in uniform. He was ready to play. So why, if Lou Mills was to be the third baseman, hold him out now? There was no reason.

Ted's argument made sense.

But he had trouble making himself believe it.

The Brewers beat the Royals, 4–3.

But for Ted the game was a personal triumph. He went 2 for 4, one of them a home run that brought in two of the Royals' runs. In the field he handled six chances without error, one of them a brilliant knockdown of a scorching line drive followed by a rifle-shot throw to first base that beat the runner by a step.

With each hit, with each successful fielding effort, the fears he had conjured up before the game faded farther and farther into the background.

By game's end, he was grinning and chattering—all

fears gone—and only the fact of the loss kept him from cheering when the last out was made and he turned toward the ramp leading to the dressing room.

In the dressing room he smiled as first Cal, and then Brian, clapped him on the shoulder and congratulated him for a good game.

Then the sportswriter with the *Kansas City Star* came across the dressing room and told him that Quincy had just announced in his office that Lou Mills would be at third base the next night.

CHAPTER
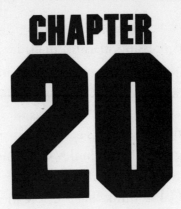

Ted was flattened.

The news hit him like a blow to the solar plexus.
He felt all the air go out of his lungs. Then he felt
his face flush red.

Could it be true?

"I'm as surprised as you," said the sports reporter.

In his shock, Ted's mind went blank. His mouth worked,
but no words came out.

The sports reporter, seeming a bit embarrassed, watched
Ted for a moment. Then he walked away, apparently
deciding against pressing him for a quote. Maybe he
thought there was nothing Ted could say.

For sure, Ted thought there was nothing he could
say.

The question came back into his mind: Could it be
true?

Certainly it was true.

Ted finished dressing in a hurry, shirt buttoned and stuffed in, trousers buckled. He grabbed his sport jacket off the hanger and, without stopping to put it on, left the dressing room.

On the way out, he kept his eyes straight ahead, hoping that the smiling face of Cal Hanley would not materialize in front of him to suggest steaks at the Happy Bull. It would be like Cal to think that a celebration dinner was in order following Ted's good night in front of the newly returned Lou Mills. But Ted knew, as presumably Cal did not, that there was nothing to celebrate. The good night in front of Lou Mills amounted to . . . zero, naught, nothing. Ted was headed back to the bench.

Outside, he leapt into the backseat of the first of the cabs lined up near the gate.

"Ted Bell?" the cabbie said, clearly pleased with the identity of his passenger.

Ted leaned back in the seat and exhaled a deep breath. "I think so," he said.

The cabbie gave Ted a puzzled look and slowly pulled away from the curb. "Where to?" he asked.

Ted did not answer immediately. Staring absently out the window, he toyed with an idea that had popped into his head unexpectedly. The idea tempted him. He could tell the cabbie to take him to the airport. He could buy a ticket on the next plane heading in the direction of Genoa—to Tulsa or Dallas or Oklahoma City, and call his parents to meet him in the car. Once home, he could issue a statement demanding that the Royals trade him.

The league-leading hitter wanted to play, not sit on the bench.

Surely there was a team that could use a strong third baseman, now a proven hitter and fielder, for the stretch drive in the pennant race.

Clearly the Kansas City Royals, under Hank Quincy, did not need Ted Bell.

"Where to?" the cabbie asked again.

Ted turned to the driver with a start, pulling himself back into the present, away from the fantasy of running away from the Royals.

He gave the cabbie the name of his hotel.

"You know?"

The voice on the telephone was Cal Hanley's.

Ted was in his hotel room, the morning sunlight streaming through the window. He was half dressed, sitting on the side of the bed, holding the telephone to his ear.

Ted did not have to ask what Cal was talking about. "Yes," he said, "I know."

"I didn't know about it until I read it in the paper this morning."

"I haven't seen a paper," Ted said flatly.

"Did Quincy tell you?"

"No. A sportswriter told me in the dressing room after the game."

Cal said, "Ouch."

"Yeah, ouch. I guess it never occurred to Quincy to mention it to me."

"I wondered why you vanished from the dressing room so quickly. I was going to invite you out for a steak."

Ted nodded unconsciously and almost smiled to himself, recalling his fear that Cal might appear in front of him before he succeeded in escaping the dressing room. "I didn't feel much like having a steak at the Happy Bull," he said.

Cal paused, and in the moment of silence Ted considered telling him how close he had come to leaving Kansas City the night before. But had he really come close to doing it? Well, he had thought about it.

Then Cal spoke. "I don't think you understand what's happening here."

Ted snorted a small laugh. "Oh, I understand, all right," he said. "The legend is back, and the rookie is returning to the bench, where he belongs."

"Now wait a minute."

"Well, that's right, isn't it?"

"I don't think so."

"Seems clear enough to me."

"Will you listen?"

Ted shrugged his shoulders, as if Cal were there to see, and said into the telephone, "Okay, sure."

"I've been around this game for a while, you know, and I've seen a lot of things happen, and I think it is perfectly clear what's happening here."

"What's that?"

"The club is going to play Lou Mills for a couple or three games—maybe four—to prove to the world that he's healthy, that he's completely recovered from the fractures. Then they'll trade him."

Ted raised an eyebrow. He rolled the thought around in his mind for a moment. The possibility had not occurred to him. Maybe Cal was right. Anything was possible. And, indeed, Cal had lived a lot of years in major league baseball. But he said, "Well, that's your theory, and you're entitled to it. It seems that everyone has a theory."

"What do you mean?"

"Brian is afraid that Quincy is going to put me at second base so he can have both Lou and me in the lineup at the same time."

Cal did not give the notion a moment's thought. "That's

nonsense," he said. Then he added, "Brian—and you, too—are looking at just the lineup. There's more involved. The Royals have two good third basemen. Make that two *great* third basemen. But no matter how great, nobody needs two of them. So the Royals are going to get rid of one of them—the older one, believe me—and receive in return something they can use in going for the pennant."

Ted hesitated. Then he said, "Maybe so."

"I don't think there's any *maybe* about it."

"But there is another theory—mine—that seems pretty likely to me," Ted said.

"What's that?"

"My theory is that Hank Quincy is determined to see me on my way to Omaha or somewhere in the minors. He didn't want me when he got me—told me as much, as a matter of fact—and he doesn't want me now."

"You're wrong."

"I guess we'll see, won't we?"

"Calm down."

"I'm calm." Ted almost smiled into the telephone. "I haven't much choice."

"In the past month you've become more than the third baseman of the future," Cal said. "You're the third baseman of the present, the right now, who's needed to spark this team into the playoffs and the World Series, and Quincy knows it." He paused. "But Quincy's got to prove that Lou is as good as new, completely recovered, in order to make a good trade."

Ted gave a small, dry laugh. "I wish you were the Royals' manager," he said.

"I'm right. Believe me."

"Then why doesn't Quincy tell me so? You're telling me but Quincy isn't. It wouldn't take more than two minutes of his valuable time."

Cal sighed into the telephone. "Hank Quincy is a strange man," he said.

"Yeah, I know," Ted said. "A genius."

"Hang in there," Cal said.

"Sure."

Ted sat through the second game of the Detroit series, a 5–1 Royals victory. Then he sat through the third game of the series, another Royals victory, this time 6–0. And he sat through the first game of a home series with the Boston Red Sox, another victory, 3–2, which boosted the Royals to within a half game of first place.

Cal had said, "Hang in there."

Ted was hanging in there.

But there were a couple of troubling facts that would not go away: Quincy had succeeded in winning with Ted Bell in a batting slump, and now Quincy was winning with Ted Bell riding the bench.

And a troubling question behind those two facts: Why

would Quincy want to change back to Ted Bell instead of Lou Mills at third base?

Why, indeed?

Lou Mills was fielding well and hitting well. He was, Ted thought time and again, a step slow running to first base, a fraction of a second slow going after a grounder. But those shortcomings were the result of age, not the injury. Clearly Lou Mills was fully recovered. And he had not left the occasional flashes of greatness on the banks of the Buffalo River in northern Arkansas.

Cal had said, "A couple or three games, maybe four," and then, if Lou Mills had demonstrated full recovery, the Royals would trade him.

It had been three games now.

But Ted saw no signs of anything changing.

The sportswriters were chewing up Quincy every day. They wrote about Ted's greatness and questioned Quincy's wisdom in playing Mills. They wrote cruelly about Mills's advancing years. One even suggested in print— and Brian flinched—that Ted Bell at second base might be a good idea.

Through all of the sportswriters' persistent questioning, Ted kept his mouth clamped shut. He had learned his lesson about being interviewed.

Hank Quincy, if concerned about the hullabaloo in the press, or Ted's frowning face, or the occasional needling shout from a fan, showed nothing. He looked and acted exactly as he always looked and acted. No different.

Ted received not so much as a nod or a glance from the manager.

And Ted did not approach Quincy. He had learned his lesson on that score, too.

Through the three games Lou Mills said little to Ted. And Ted said little to Lou Mills. What was there to say? Ted remembered his cocky question the day he joined the Royals—"Are they going to trade you or what?"— and he wasn't about to repeat that mistake.

Brian tried to boost Ted's spirits. Out of either hope or conviction—Ted did not know which—Brian overcame the newspaper story about second base and told Ted, "I think Cal is right."

They were walking through the ramp from the dugout to the dressing room after the victory over the Red Sox.

Ted managed a grin. "Well, at least it looks like your theory wasn't right," he said. "I'm on the bench, and you're on second base."

"Uh-huh. And I think that's a good indication that Cal is right."

"Oh?"

"If Quincy was going to keep you both, he'd be playing both of you. But Quincy knows that Lou is going and that you're waiting to return to third base."

Ted shrugged and said, more to himself than to Brian, "That's what everyone says—except Quincy."

Through the three games and the long, boring days of being alone in Kansas City, the idea of quitting the team and demanding a trade kept recurring in Ted's mind.

After all, if he called it quits for the season, he and the Royals would have until spring training in February to settle a new arrangement. He could get in a semester at Oklahoma State—a commitment that would please his parents—and the Royals would have months to negotiate a trade. Then, in February, he could start anew with another team—a team that wanted him.

The idea floated out in front of Ted like a piece of candy on a string that he might reach out for at any time and enjoy taking.

But he always wound up shoving the idea out of his mind.

"Hang in there," Cal kept saying.

"That's what I'm trying to do," Ted kept replying.

"Any day now," Cal said.

"Sure," Ted said.

CHAPTER 21

The day after the first game of the Boston series, Ted passed the long afternoon in a darkened and almost empty movie theater, watching John Wayne save the ranch again.

After the movie he walked back to his hotel.

It was almost time to catch a cab to the ball park, change into his uniform, take the pregame warm-up—and then sit on the bench and watch Lou Mills play third base.

A gloomy Ted Bell walked across the lobby of the hotel to pick up his room key at the front desk.

The desk clerk gave Ted two messages with his key.

Ted stepped away from the desk and looked at the first of the messages. It was from Cal—name, telephone number, and time of the call: three-thirty. Ted slipped the message into his jacket pocket. He could guess what Cal wanted: time for another pep talk.

"Hang in there," Cal would say.

"Sure," Ted would say.

And then Ted would watch Lou Mills play another game.

After three games Lou Mills's full recovery from the injury was clearly evident. He was hitting well—one home run, a double, three singles in twelve trips to the plate—and fielding well. He was healthy and able. Anyone could see that. Equally evident, Ted was sure, was the fact that Hank Quincy preferred Lou Mills to Ted Bell at third base.

Ted thought again that he should have gone home four days ago when the thought first occurred to him, or should go now, right now.

He looked at the other message—Henry Francis of the *Kansas City Star*, a telephone number, and the time of the message: ten minutes after three o'clock.

Ted frowned at the Henry Francis message. Henry Francis had written several articles criticizing Quincy for pulling Ted out of the lineup. Lou Mills was great, Henry Francis kept saying, but Ted Bell was the spark that had led the Royals upward in the standings. Undoubtedly Henry Francis was now working on another article and wanted a quote from Ted.

Ted could give Henry Francis a quote—"I'm leaving, and I demand that the Royals trade me to a club that will play me."

He shrugged at the thought, knowing he never would say the words.

Ted put the Henry Francis message in his pocket with the Cal Hanley message and walked to the bank of elevators.

In his room he sat on the side of the bed, motionless for a moment, then picked up the telephone and dialed Cal's number.

After the third ring Ted glanced at his wristwatch. A few minutes after four o'clock. Cal already might have left for the ball park. The pitcher habitually arrived early.

Then Cal answered. "Have you heard?" he asked.

"Heard what?"

"You're it. They're putting Lou up for trade."

Ted pulled the telephone away from his ear and looked at it in disbelief.

"You there?" Cal asked.

"I'm here. But what are you talking about? I mean, when—?"

"It's on the radio."

Ted felt his heart sink. "Speculation, you mean."

"No, no, no. It's for real."

"Are you sure?"

Cal laughed. "Heard it myself," he said.

"I mean, well, are you sure it's for certain?"

"It's for certain. Quincy called himself a news conference this afternoon and stood up in front of everyone and made the announcement."

"The announcement . . . " Ted still was not sure.

"He said that Ted Bell was the Royals' third baseman of the future, and that the Royals were offering Lou Mills for trade."

"I've been at a movie. I—" Ted stopped. He realized he sounded silly. "So it's really happened," he said finally.

"Maybe I should say that I told you so," Cal said.

Ted grinned into the telephone. So Cal had been right all along. "Yeah. Okay. Anything you like."

Ted was surprised by the first face he saw when he pushed open the dressing room door and walked in: Lou Mills.

In uniform but without shoes, Mills was seated on a bench, leaning back against the wall, arms folded across his chest, his feet up on a stool, chatting with Bomba Wright, who was standing over him.

The sight was puzzling to Ted.

The veteran third baseman looked neither bothered nor troubled nor angered.

He appeared relaxed and at ease with the world as he turned his face away from Bomba and toward Ted.

Had Lou Mills not heard the news?

But surely Lou Mills had heard.

Then why was he here, in uniform, casually chatting with Bomba as if nothing in the world had changed?

A chilling thought shot through Ted's mind: Cal Hanley had misunderstood the sportscast. People misunderstood radio news all the time. He would not be the first. Maybe the announcer speculated that Quincy was about to call a news conference, that Quincy then would announce Ted Bell was going to be the Royals' third baseman, and that the Royals were going to trade Lou Mills. It was possible. The speculation made sense. After all, Quincy was under a lot of pressure, from the front office and from the press. Everyone knew it. So speculation was easy. And Cal, who was listening with one ear while doing something else, misunderstood.

But there was Cal, off to Ted's left, standing in front of his stall, smiling at him.

Then Cal winked.

Beyond Cal, Brian was making a circle of his thumb and forefinger and grinning at Ted.

So Ted turned back to Lou Mills, still leaning back casually with his feet up on a stool.

"You look surprised," Mills said easily.

Bomba turned, nodded at Ted, and said, "Congratulations."

Ted said, "Thanks," and Bomba moved away, leaving the two third basemen alone together.

Ted sat on the bench next to Mills. "Surprised? Yes—
yes, I guess so."

"Really?"

"Well, I—"

"If you're surprised," Mills said, "you're the only one."

"You weren't surprised?"

"Me? I've known for weeks."

Ted blinked. "You have?"

Mills took his feet off the stool and placed them on
the floor, leaning forward. He had a small smile—sort
of sad, Ted thought—on his face. "Look," he said, "I
know how old I am. Time is running out. A man gets a
little slower—a step here, a second there." He paused.

Ted watched Mills. So he had recognized and admitted
to himself the signs of slowing down that Ted had noticed.

"I don't like it," Mills said, "but there's nothing I
can do about it." He paused again, then added, "Yes,
there is one thing that I can do about it—bow out with
grace."

Ted silently searched for the right words. Finally he
said, "But you're not finished—a long way from it!"

Mills grinned again. "Changed your mind about that,
huh?" he said.

Ted flushed, remembering his remarks in their first
meeting. "Yes," he said. "Changed my mind."

"Ah, I've had a good run at it—a good time—and I've

still got a year or two left, to help some team that hasn't yet found its Ted Bell."

"But leaving the Royals?"

"That's the one regret." He looked around the dressing room. "This team is going to the World Series. I can sense it." He turned and looked at Ted. "You're going to cheer them all the way into the World Series." He paused. "I'm going to miss being there."

"Well, I—"

Mills grinned. "Keep hollering, kid," he said. "It's good for 'em."

Ted felt a slight blush. Then he said, "Did Quincy . . . ? I mean, Quincy never said anything to me."

"You mean, did Quincy tell me?" Mills chuckled. "Of course not. Hank Quincy never tells anyone anything."

"But you said you've known for weeks."

"I knew that day in Chicago when you walked in that maybe, just maybe, my replacement had arrived. When you knocked Buster Krump's fastball out of the park, I thought, well, yes, maybe really. And then that night when I was out with a cold, I watched the game on television in the hotel and I knew it was time for ol' Lou Mills to start packing his bags."

"I never—"

"Really? You seemed pretty sure of yourself to me."

Ted shrugged and smiled slightly. "All I knew was that

I kept going back to the bench whenever you were around and healthy."

Mills laughed. "This last time, you know, Quincy was just proving that I was a healthy piece of trade bait."

"That's what Cal said," Ted said softly. "But I didn't know."

"Well, Cal was right, wasn't he?"

Ted sat for a moment without speaking. Then he said, "You're a big pair of shoes to fill."

Mills glanced at Ted. "Tell you something, kid. They say I'm a cinch to make it into the Hall of Fame. Well, if I do, I'll plan on being there the day they induct you."

Ted got to his feet. "Good luck," he said.

Mills grinned up at Ted. "You, too, Ted."

Ted had finished getting into his uniform, a process interrupted a half dozen times by teammates shaking his hand and offering congratulations.

One of the hand-shakers was Eddie Patterson. "You'll be okay," Patterson said without expression. "I knew it when you went to work on that slump, instead of acting like a crybaby."

Ted just nodded at the blank-faced veteran first baseman.

Hank Quincy came into view, making his pregame pass through the dressing room. He walked past Ted with a small nod and kept going.

"Hey!" Ted called out.

Everyone in the dressing room went silent and watched as Quincy came to a halt and slowly turned to face the person who had the impertinence to shout at the manager.

Ted was grinning.

Quincy's face was a mixture of astonishment, inquiry, and irritation.

When he had completed his turn and stood facing Ted from six feet away, Quincy squinted and said, "You talking to me?"

Ted leaned forward, hands on hips, still grinning, and said, "Why—didn't—you—tell—me?"

"Tell you what?" Quincy snapped.

Ted laughed out loud. "Nothing," he said. "Forget it."